PRAISE FOR THE JACK SIGLER SERIES
THRESHOLD

"In Robinson's latest action fest, Jack Sigler, King of the Chess Team--a Delta Forces unit whose gonzo members take the names of chess pieces--tackles his most harrowing mission yet.Threshold elevates Robinson to the highest tier of over-the-top action authors and it delivers beyond the expectations even of his fans. The next Chess Team adventure cannot come fast enough."-- **Booklist - Starred Review**

"In Robinson's wildly inventive third Chess Team adventure (after Instinct), the U.S. president, Tom Duncan, joins the team in mortal combat against an unlikely but irresistible gang of enemies, including "regenerating capybara, Hydras, Neander-thals, [and] giant rock monsters." ...Video game on a page? Absolutely. Fast, furious unabashed fun? You bet." -- **Publishers Weekly**

"Jeremy Robinson's *Threshold* is one hell of a thriller, wildly imaginative and diabolical, which combines ancient legends and modern science into a non-stop action ride that will keep you turning the pages until the wee hours. Relentlessly gripping from start to finish, don't turn your back on this book!" -- **Douglas Preston, New York Times bestselling author of Impact and Blasphemy**

"With *Threshold* Jeremy Robinson goes pedal to the metal into very dark territory. Fast-paced, action-packed and wonderfully creepy! Highly recommended!" -- **Jonathan Maberry,** *New York Times* **bestselling author of** *The King of Plagues* **and** *Rot & Ruin*

"*Threshold* is a blisteringly original tale that blends the thriller and horror genres in a smooth and satisfying hybrid mix. With his new entry in the Jack Sigler series, Jeremy Robinson plants his feet firmly on territory blazed by David Morrell and James Rollins. The perfect blend of mysticism and monsters, both human and otherwise, make *Threshold* as groundbreaking as it is riveting." -- **Jon Land**, *New York Times* bestselling author of *Strong Enough to Die*

"Jeremy Robinson is the next James Rollins."-- **Chris Kuzneski, New York Times bestselling author of The Lost Throne and The Prophecy**

"Jeremy Robinson's *Threshold* sets a blistering pace from the very first page and never lets up. This globe-trotting thrill ride challenges its well-crafted heroes with ancient mysteries, fantastic creatures, and epic action sequences. For readers seeking a fun rip-roaring adventure, look no further."
-- **Boyd Morrison, bestselling author of** *The Ark*

"Robinson artfully weaves the modern day military with ancient history like no one else."-- **Dead Robot Society**

"THRESHOLD is absolutely gripping. A truly unique story mixed in with creatures and legendary figures of mythology, technology and more fast-paced action than a Jerry Bruckheimer movie. If you want fast-paced: you got it. If you want action: you got it. If you want mystery: you got it, and if you want intrigue, well, you get the idea. In short, I $@#!$% loved this one."-- **thenovelblog.com**

"As always the Chess Team is over the top of the stratosphere, but anyone who relishes an action urban fantasy thriller that combines science and mythology will want to join them for the exhilarating Pulse pumping ride."-- **Genre Go Round Reviews**

INSTINCT

PULSE

CALLSIGN:
KING

JEREMY ROBINSON
with SEAN ELLIS

BREAKNECK MEDIA

Visit Jeremy Robinson on the World Wide Web at:
www.jeremyrobinsononline.com

Visit Sean Ellis on the World Wide Web at:
seanellisthrillers.webs.com

The Adventures of Dodge Dalton
In the Shadow of Falcon's Wings
At the Outpost of Fate

Dark Trinity: Ascendant
Magic Mirror
Secret Agent X
The Sea Wraiths
Masterpiece of Vengeance
The Scar

CALLSIGN: KING

PROLOGUE

Afar District, Ethiopia--One week ago

Moses Selassie ate alone.

This was not unusual. A solitary person by nature, Moses had never been one to seek out company, especially among those whom he considered intellectually inferior. There was no arrogance in this; he simply found conversation with most of his countrymen—gossip, facile complaints about the state of the economy, discussions about the latest football match—to be unbelievably tedious. By all rights, he should have been teaching at the University, shaping the young minds that were, in his estimation, the very future of Ethiopia...of all Africa, but instead his education and connections at the University had been able to secure him only this position: a common laborer. In Colonial times, he would have been called a 'bearer.'

Colonial times, he thought darkly. Nothing had changed. The wealth and dignity of Africa was still in the hands of outsiders. Where once there had been European monarchies, now there were multi-national corporations pillaging the natural resources of the continent and leaving only scraps for her indigenous people. He had once dreamed, like his namesake, of leading the beleaguered people of his nation to freedom from their oppressive absentee landlords. Now, those dreams were as empty as the dust that blew across the Great Rift Valley.

But tonight, he had other reasons for keeping himself apart from the two dozen or so laborers the foreigners had hired. On the previous day, he had broken with his custom by hanging on the fringes of a knot o2f idlers as they bantered about the fate of the expedition. It had been three days since anyone had come out of the cave, and tension in the camp, both among the bearers and their foreign minders, was starting to reach the boiling point.

Something has happened in there, one of the men said.

Perhaps they found something, another suggested. *Treasure?*

Moses had seen the collective reaction to that suggestion; a gleam of avarice shone from the faces of the men. It was of course very unlikely that the cave contained a trove of gold or uncut diamonds, but there were other kinds of treasure in the Rift that these men would not appreciate. Excavations in the Great Rift Valley had yielded some of the oldest remains of humankind, and many believed that the earliest ancestors of the human race had emerged here. It was exactly the sort of "treasure" that brought foreigners to the Rift; it was, he felt quite certain, the goal of this expedition. He had inquired about his new employers before leaving Addis Ababa; he doubted that a company called Nexus Genetic Research would be lured in by promises of gold or petroleum, but they would certainly have an interest in the wealth of knowledge that might be gleaned from the bones of the oldest ancestors of *Homo sapiens*.

And that was when he had made up his mind. He had to know what was in the cave.

The division of labor in the camp was explicit. Initially, their role had been to unpack and assemble the tents, and to provide logistical support in the form of cooking meals, and refueling and maintaining the generators. A few of the men had assisted in uncovering the cave entrance, but once that task was finished to the satisfaction of the research team, no laborers were permitted to leave the ad hoc compound. The meals they prepared for the researchers were shuttled to the site by the armed security team—all foreigners—and even those men were not permitted inside; the meals were left in insulated containers by the entrance.

But something was wrong. Three days had passed without anyone emerging from the cave to collect the meals.

The rumors began to flit about the camp like moths around a spotlight. Moses heard only what was said by the other bearers, but even from a distance he could see that the foreigners were likewise troubled by the situation.

Shortly after breakfast, the camp manager, accompanied by two men from the security force, approached the cave entrance, and after fifteen hesitant minutes, ventured inside. Moses surreptitiously observed the manager's assistant clinging to a handheld radio, receiving reports every few minutes until interference from the mass of earth enveloping the cavern cut off that avenue of communication. Following that, nothing. It was as if the three men had stepped through a portal to another galaxy.

The foreigners had compartmentalized their operation too well. Communications with the outside world had been restricted to the scientific team. The computers which they used to initiate a connection via the satellite dish on the edge of the camp were inside the cave, connected by several hundred meters of fiber optic cable, so the only way for the increasingly distraught assistant to seek guidance from his distant superiors was to likewise venture inside.

As the hours of the day ticked by, the fear and frustration simmered at a slow boil. Many of the Ethiopian labors were preparing to desert the camp. The security guards, evidently tipped off to the growing discontent, made a conspicuous show of force, doubling the guard on the vehicles and establishing several observation posts on the perimeter of the camp.

Though he felt no loyalty to the foreigners, Moses had no interest in deserting the camp. He was not immune to the fear of what might be happening inside that ragged slit in the hillside, but his curiosity was even more powerful. The researchers had found something in there, something important, and he wanted to know what it was.

He tried to force himself to eat everything on his plate, but the food was like sawdust in his mouth. When he could choke down no more, he threw the half-eaten meal away and wandered into the maze of tents. He did his best to appear nonchalant, which given the anxiety level in the camp was no simple feat, and charted a course that brought him to the edge of the compound closest to the cave entrance. Two thick cables—one to deliver electrical power, the other the fiber-optic line—snaked out from the camp, reaching across the emptiness to disappear into the barely visible gap in the hillside. Moses fixated on the insulated bundles; they would mark his path into the cave.

Although the security force had been largely redeployed to watch for deserters, the primary focus of the expedition—the cave itself—had not been abandoned. Two guards were posted at the edge of the camp. To the west, the sun was just kissing the horizon, casting its rays sidelong across the landscape, and Moses knew he would never get a better chance. Taking a deep breath, he emerged from his place of concealment and began striding toward the nearest guard post.

He could see the security man squinting into the sunset in a futile effort to identify him, and offered a friendly wave. The guard hesitated, as if reluctant to let go of the assault rifle he held at the low ready, but raised his right hand to return the greeting. For Moses, that casual gesture was the signal to go.

He bolted forward, running directly at the guard, and closed the distance before the confused man could even think about dropping his hand back to the pistol grip of his weapon. Moses bowled into him, knocking the man backward into the uncoiled nest of concertina wire that ringed the camp. Because he was anticipating the impact, Moses recovered quickly. Using the stunned guard like a stepping stone, he launched himself over the wire.

The second guard, half-blinded by the setting sun, did not immediately grasp that his comrade had been subdued, but when he heard the sound of footsteps out in the open, he knew something was wrong. Moses heard a shouted warning but paid it no heed. Instead, he aimed himself at the twinned cables and started running as if his life depended on it; in fact, it did.

He'd only gone a few steps when the report of a gun, shattered the silence. Then the sound repeated again. And again.

But no bullets found him and after only a few seconds he saw the cave entrance clearly against the hillside, only fifty meters away...and then thirty meters...and then, almost abruptly, he was inside.

He did not linger there to congratulate himself. He didn't think the security men would come in after him, but their bullets might. He kept running, barely even looking at this new subterranean environment, until the only sound he could hear was his own pounding heartbeat.

As the initial surge of adrenaline drained away, his legs turned to rubber. He sagged against the smooth wall of the cave and struggled to bring his breathing under control. After a few moments, when he was certain that he was not being pursued, he pushed away from the wall and took his first look at his surroundings.

He had never been in a cave before, but this one was nothing like his expectations. Although the entrance that he and the other laborers had helped uncover in the early days of the expedition, before being confined to the camp, was just large enough to admit one person at a time, the tunnel into the hillside was considerably larger. Moses reckoned that it was big enough to accommodate a truck.

The interior of the cave was illuminated by a chain of drop

lights, suspended from pitons that had been hammered into the wall. The bulbs cast their light on bare stone; there were no calcium formations or phosphorescent lichens, no pools of seepage, only dust and dry rock. But there were sounds in the distance, the noise of human activity, deeper underground. Moses resumed his journey.

The passage wended back and forth, descending on a steep grade, and then abruptly opened into an enormous chamber. The incandescent light bulbs revealed only a fraction of the immense cavern, but from what he could see, Moses guessed it might be large enough to contain a football stadium. But that was only the first surprise.

Unlike the passage, this chamber was not empty. The floor was covered in what looked, at first glance, like enormous pillars of white stone.

"Bones," Moses whispered. Not human bones, but the skeletal remains of much larger animals. Thousands of skeletons, many still adorned with a sheath of desiccated tissue, were piled up deep on the floor of the vast cavern, as far as the eye could see and the electric lights could reveal.

Along one nearby wall, he saw large plastic cargo cases stacked in an orderly row, and nearby a series of folding tables with laptop computers and other electronic devices, but the screens were dark and there was no sign of the research team. As he made a cursory examination of the equipment, Moses realized that someone had cleared a path, leading into the heart of tangled nest of bones. The noise he had heard earlier was coming from somewhere along that path.

The bones rose up on either side of Moses as he advanced toward the disturbance, shrouding the way ahead in shadows, but there was enough ambient light to guide him along. After about forty meters, the path opened onto a large circular clearing, and there Moses found the source of the noise. His eyes were drawn to the movement, and after a few moments he could distinguish the familiar features of the scientists who had gone into the cave several days before, five men and two women. They were working among the bones, but their activity didn't look like careful research. They were building

There were ten originally, Moses thought. *Where are the rest?*

Something had gone very wrong in the cave and Moses intuitively recognized that the people he saw were either the victims of some terrible tragedy, or were its perpetrators. He held back, observing them, without drawing attention to himself.

The seven researchers moved like automatons. Their faces, haggard and drawn, were expressionless. They rooted in the bones, casting most of what they grasped aside, but occasionally they would take their discoveries to the center of the clearing and add it to the strange structure that was taking shape there. Moses edged forward to get a better look.

It's a temple, he thought. *A shrine. But to what?*

Driven by curiosity, he risked moving into the open. He needn't have worried. One of them passed within arm's reach after having placed a smooth curved bone on the shrine; the man's eyes did not even flicker in his direction. The laboring researchers were oblivious to his presence, and indeed to any external stimuli. Nothing mattered to them except the bones.

Moses knelt at the shrine and peered inside. An eighth researcher lay there, arms crossed and hugging something to her chest, but otherwise, unmoving...dead? No, he detected the gentle rise of the woman's breast with each breath.

He recognized her instantly: Dr. Felice Carter, one of the geneticists, and the only black member of the research team. He didn't think she was African—probably an American, descended from African slaves taken across the ocean centuries before—but the mere fact of her skin color awakened in him a sense of kinship. Without quite knowing why, he reached into the curious construct of bones....

No, not bones, he thought, and in a rush of understanding he realized what the cave was.

…and pulled the unconscious woman into his embrace.

The noise stopped.

As he hefted Felice onto his shoulder, Moses saw that the other researchers had abruptly stopped digging in the bone pile and were now all facing the shrine. Their eyes were still devoid of expression, but they were, unmistakably, looking at him.

Moses ran.

One of the men stood between him and the path through the bones, but Moses did not hesitate. He lowered his unburdened left shoulder and charged, bowling the man backward into the bone pile. Moses recovered without stumbling and resumed his flight, but through the sound of his own footsteps and the rush of blood in his ears, he could hear the others close behind.

His journey out of the bone chamber and through the tunnel passage seemed to take only a few seconds, yet at every step he felt certain that the men and women giving chase would catch him. Only as he exited the cave did it occur to him that he might be in even more danger outside, where the security force with their assault rifles would no doubt be waiting. Trusting that they would check their fire when they saw that he carried Felice, he quickened his pace.

But no one was waiting for him outside the cave entrance. The expected confrontation with the guards did not occur. Their attention was consumed by the riot that had broken out in the camp.

Evidently, the sound of shots being fired at Moses had been enough to light the fuse on the powder keg of discontent among the laborers. Perhaps believing that the security guards were beginning to execute some of their comrades, the bearers had unleashed a campaign of destruction. Thick columns of smoke rose into the twilit evening sky, marking the location of tents that were now being consumed by flames. A dull roar— shouts and screams—rolled across the floor of the Rift, punctuated by periodic gunshots.

Moses paused for just a moment, but a glance over his shoulder confirmed that the mindless pursuers were still coming, and faced with what seemed like two equally bad choices, Moses elected to brave the chaos in the camp.

The guards he had passed on his initial egress were gone. Moses could see figures moving in the haze of smoke, but no one took note of him as he entered the camp and made his way through the wreckage.

His goal was the parking area where the expedition's vehicles had been sitting idle for more than a week, but when he got there, his hopes of a quick escape evaporated. Several of his fellow bearers apparently had the same idea, and they were armed with captured rifles. Gathering the last shreds of his courage, Moses approached one of the armed men.

"Please. You must give us a ride."

Another man, leaning against the front fender of a dust streaked Land Cruiser, evidently the leader of the impromptu gang, shouted: "Of course you may ride with us. Five hundred thousand birr. For each of you."

It was an obscene amount of money, and the man surely knew that none of the bearers possessed even a fraction of that, but Moses felt a glimmer of hope. "She is one of their scientists. Her company will pay what you ask."

The gang leader grinned, but before the deal could be finalized, a disturbance behind them caused the armed bearers to brandish their weapons. Moses turned and saw the haggard forms of the scientists from the cave charging toward them.

One of the gunmen shouted a warning and jabbed his weapon meaningfully at the approaching horde, but the researchers, in the grip of some primal fury, did not show the least sign of being intimidated. They swarmed around the vehicles, and in the space of a heartbeat, overwhelmed the gang.

Not a single shot was fired. The rifles, taken from the security force, had already been fired empty. Nevertheless, the attacking group seemed to recognize their deadly potential.

With preternatural strength they wrenched the weapons from the hands of the gang, and then commenced bludgeoning the would-be extortionists.

Moses had witnessed a fair amount of violence in his life, but nothing like this. The crunch of bones being shattered and the wet squish of organs rupturing were an assault on his senses. The savagery left him stunned for a moment, so stunned in fact that he almost failed to grasp that he and Felice remained untouched.

Why aren't they attacking me? Attacking us?

He had the good sense not to let the opportunity slip away. He crossed to the nearest Land Cruiser and climbed into its spacious rear seating area. Only when the door was closed behind him did he shift Felice off his shoulder. Without missing a beat, he crawled through the space between the front seats and settled in behind the steering wheel. Thankfully, the key was in the ignition. He gave it a twist and felt a wave of relief as the engine turned over.

It was a short-lived emotion. He looked up and found that the researchers had left off their grisly task and were now pressed close against the windows of the Land Cruiser, peering inside.

It's her, Moses realized. *They're protecting her.*

But that wasn't quite right. He recalled the shrine they had been building around her. They weren't her guardians; they were her worshippers, and they weren't about to let him steal their goddess away.

Let them try and stop me.

Moses punched the accelerator pedal. The SUV shot forward, knocking three of the scientists aside. The interior reverberated with the noise of fists and rifle butts striking fenders and glass, but there was little they could do to prevent his escape. Like an unstoppable juggernaut, the Land Cruiser rolled over or shoved aside everything and everyone in its path until, with almost anticlimactic ease, the rubble of the camp fell behind in the distance and was swallowed up by the night.

>>>CDC Team led by Sara Fogg en route to primary site. Fogg holds degrees in molecular biology, genetics and biochemistry. Simulation indicates probability of successfully engineering a vaccine is 53.3%

53%??? That's not very encouraging.

>>>Simulations incorporating other CDC teams yielded 39.7%, 36.2%, and 28.8% probability of success, respective-ly. Fogg's team has the highest likelihood of delivering the desired outcome.

Whatever you say.

>>>Be advised. Fogg issued an unauthorized personal communication prior to departure.

Who did she call?

>>>A text message was sent to Jack Sigler, last known residence: Fort Bragg, North Carolina.

Military?

>>>Accessing....

>>>Sigler's military record has been redacted. The most recent unclassified entry, dated January 2006, lists him as a platoon leader in the 6th Ranger Battalion.

Great. That means he's a spook. Some kind of black ops guy.

>>>There is an 82.5% probability that Sigler is still actively serving in the US military and currently operating in a clan-destine capacity.

What's his relationship to Fogg? What did she tell him?

GAMBIT

1.

Addis Ababa, Ethiopia

Four men were sent to kill King.

Of course they didn't think of him as "King." They knew his name was Jack Sigler, but even that meant nothing to them. He was just the target. If they had known about his callsign, identifying him as part of the ultra-secret and ultra-lethal black ops group called Chess Team, they probably would have sent forty.

△ △ △

King settled into the cracked vinyl seat in the taxi's rear passenger area, and just for a moment, closed his eyes. He was tired, but strangely his fatigue was not the product of sustained physical or even mental effort. In fact, he thrived on exertion.

This capacity had served him particularly well in his military service, enabling him to surmount whatever challenges training or combat placed before him, whether it was negotiating a twelve-mile nighttime land nav course, or taking down the deadliest terrorists in the world. His ability to turn the tables on exhaustion had been instrumental in his success as the leader of Chess Team, a small but very elite group of operators drawn from the ranks of the US military's Joint Special Operations Command, and now recently given special autonomy to defend the nation—indeed, the entire world—from threats that were beyond the comprehension of traditional military forces. They took their operational callsigns from the chessboard. As leader, he was naturally "King." Zelda Baker, the first woman to battle her way up through the male-dominated world of Spec-Ops, was "Queen." Erik Somers, Iranian by birth, but 110% an American patriot—the extra ten percent owed to a physique that would have been the envy of Schwarzenegger in his prime—was "Bishop." The Korean, Shin Dae-jung was "Knight," and "Rook" was reserved for Stan Tremblay....

King sighed. Rook was presently missing in action, presumed dead by many of those who knew the circumstances of his final mission, and that was surely a contributing factor to his weariness. So also was his recent discovery that his parents—his loving mother, and the father who had walked out on both of them years before—were in fact Russian sleeper agents, actively engaged in an operation directed against Chess Team. Their subsequent disappearance, and the knowledge that they were still out there, working against him, was a burden King carried alone. And if that wasn't enough, he'd somehow become the foster father to Fiona Lane, a thirteen year old orphan whose knowledge of an ancient divine language had made her both very powerful and a target for kidnapping or assassination. At first, King's mission had been to protect her, but he'd since grown to love the girl as his own. Officially, Fiona Lane no longer existed. After Chess Team rescued her, and became a black op, she came with them. That didn't make being her father any easier. He sometimes thought taking down terrorist cells was less work.

But the true source of his weariness was that he was tired down to his bones because of inactivity. He had spent most of the last twenty hours in the cramped confines of passenger jets, interspersed with equally interminable periods of waiting in ticketing and security checkpoint lines, all the while plagued by the possibility that Sara might be in danger.

Sara Fogg was King's girlfriend.

The term felt alien to King. He had never had much success with relationships. None had ever lasted more than a few months, but he and Sara had been an item since working together on a critical Chess Team mission to Viet Nam in 2010, where her unique abilities as a "disease detective" for the Centers for Disease Control and Prevention had literally saved the human race from extinction.

Theirs was not, suffice it to say, a traditional relationship.

He ran a hand through his unruly black hair then opened his eyes and took out his phone. The display screen told him what he already knew—"service unavailable"—but what he was interested in was stored in the device's memory: Sara's text message to him:

Safari time. Got a hot one ;-) Every THing Is Ok. Pizza In A week or so.

"A hot one" undoubtedly signified a disease outbreak; epidemiologists referred to an area where a contagion was spreading as a "hot zone." The rest of the message seemed innocuous enough.

Or at least it would to anyone who didn't know Sara Fogg very well.

King had seen the text for what it was almost immediately. The message was anything but typical for the erudite, precise and detail-oriented disease detective. Sara would never send a missive so riddled with apparent formatting errors, at least not without a very good reason.

The simple fact of the message itself was very telling. Once a CDC response team was activated, its members were not supposed to communicate with the outside world. As team leader, Sara knew this better than anyone, so for her to break protocol, even in such a seemingly harmless manner, was a veritable cry for help. The kind of help that only Chess Team could provide.

Also, Sara never, ever used smileys.

It had only taken about fifteen seconds for him to decipher her hasty code. The capital letters following the emoticon spelled out: ETHIOPIA. That was absolutely not an accident. The code wasn't very sophisticated, but it probably would have slipped past an automated eavesdropping program like the NSA's massive Echelon system. And so within a minute of receiving the text, King was on the move.

He had made a conscious decision to deal with this on his own. Most of the Chess Team members were otherwise occupied anyway, but with nothing more to go on than a cryptic text message and a bad feeling, he was loath to utilize the many other assets that were available for discretionary use. That included Deep Blue.

King may have been the head of Chess Team, but Deep Blue was its central nervous system. When the group had first been mustered, they had believed the mysterious Deep Blue— the code name was an homage to the computer that had defeated chess champion Gary Kasparov in the 1990's—to be a cyber-warrior with a Spec-Ops background and almost unlimited information resources. Only later did they learn the man's real identity: then-President of the United States, Tom Duncan. The leader of the free world, a former Army Ranger, had been moonlighting as the eyes, ears and guiding hand of Chess Team. A recent crisis had forced Duncan to sacrifice his presidency in order to save the country, but that hadn't spelled the end of his association with Chess Team. With a few strokes of the keyboard, Deep Blue probably could have arranged for supersonic transport to Africa, and put King on the ground in Ethiopia inside of three hours, armed to the teeth and ready for anything.

But if Sara had wanted that, she would have come right out and said it. King wasn't entirely convinced that her message had been intended to summon him. She might simply have been saying: 'Keep an eye on me.' King had decided to split the difference.

So, instead of parachuting in from a stealth aircraft in black BDU's, sporting an XM-25 airburst delivery weapon, his favorite SiG P220 .45 caliber semi-automatic pistol and his 7-inch fixed blade KA-BAR knife, King was riding in a battered Toyota Corolla taxicab, wearing a black Elvis T-shirt and blue jeans, with nothing more in his go-bag than a change of clothes, some travelling money, and a phone with a service plan that didn't extend to Ethiopia. But that didn't mean he was without resources. Chess Team had contacts in every part of the world, and his phone also contained a list of suppliers—some reputable, some not so much—who could provide him with almost anything he needed on very short notice. A discreet inquiry made during a layover in Germany had revealed that the CDC team planned to establish a command center at Tewahedo General Hospital in Addis Ababa; in fact, they would have only just arrived. The drive from Bole International Airport to the hospital would take about thirty minutes. King reckoned that inside of an hour, he'd be ready for anything.

That was an hour more than he got.

△ △ △

One of the first lessons every soldier learned was the importance of situational awareness, or as drill instructors were fond of saying: "Keep your head on a swivel." Even in the absence of a perceived threat, it was almost second nature for King to crane

his head around for a 360° sweep every few minutes, scrutiniz-
ing the faces of passersby, the shadowy recesses of alleyways, and
the way other cars moved through traffic. The first sign of
trouble might not be obvious, just something about a scene that
wasn't quite right.

The pair of black Dodge Ram pick-ups charging up behind the taxi, however, were pretty hard to miss.

"No way."

The black trucks certainly stood out from the other cars
King had seen since arriving, but the reason they commanded
his attention owed to the fact that he had seen similar vehicles
roaming the streets of Baghdad and Kandahar—trucks with
darkened bullet-resistant glass and concealed armor plating,
driven by private security contractors.

Got to be a coincidence, he thought. Security contractors—
mercenaries, in more common parlance—were ubiquitous in
developing countries, working as bodyguards for wealthy
businessmen, or training military and police forces.

His belief that there was a rational explanation lasted about
ten seconds—the length of time it took for the lead truck to
race ahead and pull alongside the taxi. As it did, the passenger
side window slid down.

"Look out!"

Even as he shouted the warning, King curled himself into a
ball behind the driver's seat. An instant later he heard a sound
like hammers striking metal followed by the distinctive crack of
shattering glass, but the report of the gunfire was conspicuously
absent. There was a rush of air through the cab and the noise of
an engine roaring past. He risked a quick look.

All the windows on the driver side had been shattered and
the tempered glass of the windshield was now fogged with
myriad tiny cracks. King saw the truck that had strafed the cab
a few hundred meters ahead, while the second remained close on
their tail. He then turned his attention to the driver.

"Are you..." He didn't bother finishing the inquiry. The

Ethiopian man lay slumped over the steering wheel, his head and back a mess of red.

King breathed a curse at the senselessness of the murder, and then another when he realized that the cab was now veering out of control toward the edge of the road.

Even though it meant risking exposure, he knew he had to keep the car on the pavement; if it crashed, then he was dead anyway. He thrust his upper torso over the back of the driver's seat, shoving the slain driver out of the way with one hand, and gripping the steering wheel with the other. He steered the cab away from disaster, but this minor victory did little to cheer him. The cab was losing speed and the two pick-ups had him boxed in. It was only a matter of time before they checkmated him.

Where's Chess Team when I really need them?

He pushed that idea right out of his head. Defeatism was a self-fulfilling prophecy. Maybe he didn't have the team to back him up, but that was no reason to give in to despair. Maybe it was true that the king was the least effective, most vulnerable piece on the chessboard, but his callsign didn't define him or his abilities.

Still, it would have been nice to have Rook next to him, blasting away with his Desert Eagle pistols.

Prioritize, he told himself. *First order of business, get control of this vehicle.*

He manhandled the driver's dead weight over onto the passenger's seat, and then without letting go of the wheel, crawled over the back of the seat. By the time he finally got his legs onto the pedals, the Corolla was down to about 30 km/h—he could sprint faster than that. He cast a glance over his shoulder and saw the trailing pick-up hurtling toward him like a tsunami. King stomped the accelerator to the floor.

The engine revved loudly with the infusion of gasoline, but for a few seconds, the car refused to gain speed. Just as it was grudgingly beginning to cooperate, King's head abruptly snapped back against the headrest. The charging truck had rear-ended him, hard.

A sharp pain shot through King's neck, but he gritted his teeth through it and maintained steady pressure on the gas pedal. The driver of the pursuing Dodge had probably been hoping that the bump would send the Corolla spinning out of control, but instead it acted like the catapult on an aircraft carrier, launching the cab forward and giving it enough momentum to actually start accelerating again.

It was another small—too small—victory. King was still vastly outmatched. His unknown enemies had all the advantages. As he maintained steady pressure on the accelerator, the speedometer needle creeping past 100 km/h, he took quick stock of what he had to work with in order to mount an effective counter-attack.

It was a very short list.

He tore a hole through the damaged windshield to get an unobscured view of the road ahead. The lead truck was braking, slowing down and dominating the center of the road to prevent him from passing. The side mirror showed him the grill of the trailing truck, looming large once more as it closed in for another bump. It was safe to assume that the drivers were coordinating their actions; King knew that his only hope lay in unpredictability.

He steered to the right side of the road. The pick-up immediately moved right in order to block him.

King swerved to the left, and again the truck did, too.

He did this twice more, testing the driver's reaction time, and more importantly, getting familiar with the Corolla's capabilities. The vehicle was not in the best shape, but thus far he'd seen no indication that it was on the verge of breaking down. The temperature gauge showed the engine running hot—not too hot yet, but he didn't want to take the chance of it failing at a critical moment. He turned the heater on full blast, venting some of the heat into the car's interior. With the windows shot out, he barely noticed.

He steered left again, all the way to the edge of the road. The truck followed suit. He then swerved right, exactly as he had before, putting the Corolla in what he hoped was the lead truck's blind spot. The driver of the pick-up took the bait, pulling all the way to the right in order to prevent King from passing on that side.

King shifted the automatic transmission out of overdrive and stomped the gas pedal. Even as the truck was moving right, King steered left. The taxi surged ahead closing the gap before the other driver could react.

King kept one eye on the pick-up as the Corolla pulled alongside it. He caught a glimpse of the driver—a Caucasian man—snarling in frustration as he hauled the steering wheel left to cut King off, but he was too late. The taxi slipped past the Dodge. King had escaped their killing box.

He didn't waste time congratulating himself. His situation was just marginally better than it had been thirty seconds earlier. His only hope lay in finding a way to lose his pursuers, and that meant getting off the highway where the trucks had the advantage of superior horsepower. With one eye on the road, he took out his phone.

Before leaving home, he had downloaded a city map of Addis Ababa. It wasn't quite as useful as a live GPS, but it was better than nothing. He dragged his finger around the touch screen until he found the airport, and from there, was able to guess his present position, moving northeast along Ring Road, the major highway that circled the city.

The area near the airport was sparsely inhabited, with few access roads, but a more developed section of the city lay ahead. If he could make it there…get lost in the maze of surface streets and buildings…he just might have a chance.

If, he thought grimly.

The sound of hammer blows reverberated through the taxi's frame and King ducked as bullets plucked at the upholstery of the seat beside him. He felt something tug at his right arm and a moment later his biceps started burning. He didn't look; his arm was still working, so it probably wasn't anything more than a graze, and besides, there wasn't anything he could do about it.

Then he realized, almost too late, that the shots had been a diversion. When he had ducked down instinctively, it had given the pick-up's driver a chance to close in. The protective bumper guard that wrapped around the Ram's front end filled the side mirror as the truck sidled up next to him.

In a rush of understanding, King realized that the other driver was trying to spin him. It was a technique taught in tactical driving courses; a carefully delivered hit to the rear wheel of a fleeing car could force it to spin around 180°, at which point the car's momentum would be pulling against the direction of the drive wheels, causing the vehicle to stall instantly.

I took that class, too, asshole!

When the pick-up's driver made his move, King was ready. As the Dodge veered toward him, he hit the brakes. The taxi was no longer where the driver of the pursuing truck thought it would be, but he had already committed himself to the maneuver. The truck swerved across the lane in front of the taxi, even as King accelerated again, steering the opposite direction to swing around on the other side.

It almost worked.

A crunch of metal shuddered through the taxi as the truck's rear tire hooked the front end of the Corolla, and suddenly both vehicles were locked together, rolling over and over down the length of the road in a spectacular dance of mutual self-destruction.

2.

Sara Fogg hated traveling.

Perhaps "hate" was too strong a word. If her antipathy had been that strong, she surely would have chosen a different line of work.

Most of what she did as an infectious disease investigator for the CDC took place in the relatively safe confines of the laboratory, but like any other war, the battle to stop disease outbreaks before they could blossom into epidemics required her to be present on the front lines, and that meant travel, usually to unfamiliar and often remote locations around the world.

That, in and of itself, did not bother her. She wasn't the least bit xenophobic; the world was a veritable buffet of diverse cultures, and she treasured each unique new encounter...well, most of them. Sara's dislike for world travel and her preference for lab work, derived from a condition known as Sensory Processing Dysfunction, specifically a type of the disorder called Sensory Discrimination Disorder.

Normally, when a person receives sensory input, the signals travel from the sensory organs—eyes, ears, nose—to various parts of the brain where the stimuli is processed and reconciled with information already stored in that person's memory. Smells and sounds and sights are compared with things that person has already experienced, and a sympathetic response is triggered. The smell of baking cookies might stimulate a person's appetite. A loud noise might cause a release of adrenaline. But for someone with Sensory Discrimination Disorder, the nervous impulses don't go where they're supposed to. They might hear smells, or experience a seemingly unrelated physical reaction when exposed to a particular visual or auditory stimulus.

Because she had lived with it all her life, Sara didn't really see her SDD as a liability. Indeed, it gave her an advantage in certain situations. Her heightened sensory abilities had saved her life during a mission with Jack Sigler and his team—several times, in fact—and when she had later been temporarily "cured" by exposure to an unusual quartz crystal, she had felt an acute sense of loss. Sometimes, she almost thought of the disorder as a "superpower." But that didn't make dealing with it in on a day-to-day basis any easier.

She had developed effective strategies for coping in the familiar environs of her home and at the CDC headquarters in Atlanta where she did most of her work, but going out into the field was always a challenge. Invariably, she would be exposed to a host of unfamiliar stimuli, and there was no predicting just how her nervous system would react.

She took a deep breath, bracing herself for the worst, then exhaled and opened the door of the rented SUV.

Addis Ababa was relatively modern. Despite the fact that some of the first humans on the planet had probably lived in Ethiopia, the city had only been founded in the late nineteenth century, and its founder, Emperor Menelik II, had envisioned it as an Imperial capital. Because of its remote location and relatively sparse resources, the city had not grown organically like most cities in the developing world, with small villages of farmers gradually coalescing around an urban core. Instead, it had immediately become a center for education and other professional endeavors. Nevertheless, the economic hardships that persistently plagued the region—the entire continent, really—had intensified the flood of migrants from rural areas into the city. Poverty was endemic, and despite the efforts of the government, some of the streets through which the CDC team had passed were thick with beggars. But unlike many cities in the developing world, the roads were paved and there wasn't a camel, ox, or donkey to be seen.

Sara took a cautious breath, but the expected sensory onslaught did not occur. There were sounds—traffic on the streets around the hospital—and smells—vehicle exhaust and something else...eucalyptus trees, she realized—but these weren't unfamiliar to her.

So far, so good. She caught a glimpse of her reflection in the SUV's window. With her spiky dark hair and trim, athletic physique, she didn't look like most people's idea of a lab rat. At least she didn't look as tired or anxious as she felt.

"Doctor Fogg?"

She turned to find a nervous looking Asian man, wearing short-sleeves and khakis, approaching her vehicle. "I'm Sara Fogg."

"I am Dr. Hideoshi Nakamura, with the World Health Organization." The man smiled, but his anxiety did not abate. "I am pleased to welcome you. But I will confess, I am uncertain why you have come."

That caught Sara by surprise. When the CDC activated an investigative team to respond to an international incident, it was almost always at WHO's instigation. "Uncertain? I don't understand. Didn't you request our help?"

"I know of no such request. The patient you inquired about...there is no evidence that she has contracted a contagious disease."

"That's my fault." A new voice intruded, someone from heartland America, judging by the accent. Sara turned to greet the newcomer and saw a Caucasian man moving toward her, flashing a roguish smile. She thought he looked kind of like a young Harrison Ford—*no*, she amended, *he looks like Han Solo*. He quickened his step until he reached her, and thrust out a hand. "I'm Max Fulbright. Sorry about the confusion, but it was me that called you here."

Sara warily accepted his handclasp. "Dr. Fulbright, is it? I think you owe us an explanation."

"Oh, I'm not a doctor." Fulbright's smile never slipped. "I work out of the embassy, cultural attaché."

Sara resisted the urge to roll her eyes. "Cultural attaché" was usually a euphemism for "spy." But if Fulbright was indeed a CIA officer—if the Central Intelligence Agency had a special interest in what might be an unidentified contagion—then it confirmed the suspicions that had plagued her from the beginning. From the moment the call came in, something about this incident had seemed off. She hadn't been able to pin down exactly what it was, but her anxiety had prompted her to bend the rules just enough to send Jack Sigler a text message.

"The patient," Fulbright continued, "is an American citizen. That's how I got involved."

"Dr. Nakamura just told me that there's no evidence of infectious disease," Sara countered, unmoved by his smile or his evident sincerity. "And he's imminently more qualified than you to make that judgment. Do you have any idea how costly it is to spin up a CDC response team? And, what if there's a real outbreak somewhere, while we're here running down your false alarm? Lives could be lost. Mr. Fulbright, didn't your mother ever tell you the story of the little boy who cried wolf?"

"With all due respect to Dr. Nakamura," Fulbright gave a polite bow to the WHO representative, "I'd appreciate a second opinion. And Dr. Fogg, as you'll recall, in the end, there really was a wolf."

Sara sighed then glanced over her shoulder to where her team was already unpacking their gear. "Kerry, find out where they want us to set up."

Kerry Frey was a compact man in his fifties, with a kindly face and glasses that made him look like an absent-minded professor instead of one of the world's leading virologists. He was also Sara's assistant in charge of personnel. Frey nodded and immediately headed for the hospital entrance.

Sara turned back to Fulbright. "Just because there's smoke doesn't mean there's fire, but once the firemen arrive, they have to check it out anyway. You got us here, Fulbright, so that's what we're going to do: check it out."

"I couldn't hope for anything more."

Sara shook her head in resignation, and then joined the rest of her team as they unpacked their rented vehicles. The team moved with practiced efficiency, shuttling the heavy plastic cases containing their portable lab equipment into the hospital. Everyone in the team knew exactly what their job was; her role as team leader did not excuse Sara from pack mule duty. The first priority in any outbreak situation was establishing the command center and laboratory facilities, and that meant everyone had to pitch in to get the equipment up and running. In this case, the area designated for their use was a conference room on the first floor of the hospital.

The second priority was to assess the infected patient.

While Frey and the rest of the team started breaking out computer hardware, Sara began donning a one-piece, single-use Level A hazmat suit, made from disposable Tyvek.

"Can I get one of those?"

Sara realized that Fulbright had followed her team into the conference room. Dr. Nakamura was nowhere to be seen.

"Sorry, none to spare." She resisted the impulse to make a dig about his lack of any kind of meaningful qualifications. She'd already made her point, and given the size of Fulbright's ego, it seemed likely that further comment on that subject would just bounce right off the man.

As she pulled the suit around her shoulders, leaving the

headgear off for the moment, Nakamura entered the room, accompanied by a handsome bearded black man wearing a white lab coat. The WHO representative made the introduction. "This is Dr. Abdullah. He has been treating the patient."

Abdullah's eyes drifted to the hazmat suit and he swallowed nervously. "When we heard you were coming, we moved her—Miss Carter, the patient—to an isolation room on the fourth floor, but… We have very limited resources here."

Sara surmised that the Ethiopian doctor was probably wondering if he had unknowingly contracted some horrible virus. "The suits are just a precautionary measure. I'm sure they're not necessary, but I have to follow our protocol."

The doctor nodded, evincing a measure of relief.

Sara grabbed a specimen collection kit. "I'd like to see her right away."

"Of course." He gestured for her to follow. Not surprisingly, Fulbright joined them as if he had every right to. As they walked, Abdullah brought Sara up to date on the patient's history. "The patient was brought to us three days ago. We haven't been able to ascertain the identity of the man who dropped her off. She was catatonic, but clearly suffering from dehydration."

"How did you identify her?"

"She wore a badge from a research firm; Nexus Genetics. We were able to learn that she was part of an expedition to the Afar region—the Great Rift Valley. Nexus has not been forthcoming with information about Miss Carter or the purpose of the expedition."

"Geneticists doing field research in the Rift Valley?" Sara didn't like the sound of that. She made a mental note to check up on Nexus at the earliest opportunity. "I suppose there's a chance they might have been exposed to something contagious, but that's a pretty remote area. If she's picked up something, she would have got it from an animal or possibly a windborne vector. Possibly a bacillus or fungal spore. I doubt we're looking at anything communicable.

"But," she added, as they filed into an elevator car, "it is more probable that it's just a case of dehydration. How is she responding to therapy?"

Abdullah pressed a button on the control panel. "Her vital signs have improved. Blood tests confirm that her organs are functioning properly, and her white blood cell count is normal. However, she has not regained consciousness."

"Was she injured?" Even as she asked, Sara knew that there was a much more likely explanation: psychological trauma.

Abdullah confirmed her suspicions. "I believe her condition may be psychosomatic. When she arrived, she was holding an object—clinging to it, like a lifeline. When we tried to take it from her, she became agitated, almost to the point of cardiac arrest. We decided to let her keep it."

"What object?"

The elevator car settled to a stop and the doors slid open. Sara's senses were immediately hit with the smell unique to hospitals—a mixture of sickness and heavy duty disinfectant that grew stronger as they moved through the hallway. It was a like a siren, blaring in her head, but Abdullah's answer shocked her out of her sensory fugue.

"A skull. An ape skull, I think."

Sara almost gasped aloud. A primate skull in the hands of a geneticist suspected of being a carrier for an unknown contagion? Now she was certain that Fulbright knew more than he was letting on, and suddenly wearing the hazmat suit didn't seem quite so unnecessary.

But there was a piece that still didn't fit. "I didn't know there were apes in that part of the Rift Valley."

"I don't believe there are. But the skull looks very old. A fossil, perhaps. As I said, she became agitated when we tried to take it away, so we have left it alone." He stopped at a closed door, but made no move to enter. "This is her room."

There was a sign taped to the door, and even though she

couldn't read Amharic, Sara had a pretty good idea what it said. Ideally, there should have been a number of other contamination control measures—a negative air pressure system, rubber seals on the door, plastic sheeting at the very least—but as both Abdullah and Nakamura had stated, there was no reason to believe that the patient was sick with a contagious disease. She nodded to the men, and then tugged the suit's cowl over her head and zippered herself in. The hospital odor vanished as oxygen began to flow from the suit's self-contained breathing apparatus. All three men conspicuously took a step back as she reached for the door handle.

Beyond that portal was an ordinary hospital room. A tall, dark-skinned woman, covered in a simple white sheet, lay supine upon a very ordinary hospital bed. Sara listened to the gentle hiss of air in her suit for a moment, waiting to see if the woman would stir—she did not—then moved forward.

Her eyes were drawn immediately to the object the woman held protectively to her breast. Through the patient's splayed fingers, Sara was able to make out that it was indeed a skull, and that it was certainly not human; the heavy brow ridges and flatter aspect seemed to verify Dr. Abdullah's supposition that it belonged to an ape, but it was beyond the scope of Sara's knowledge to identify the species. The skull was discolored with age, almost certainly something unearthed many centuries after the animal it had once been part of had died, but it did not automatically follow that the skull was harmless. Some viruses could remain dormant for long periods, just waiting for exposure to a new host. Sara decided that, regardless of whether a pathogen could be identified from the patient's labs, the skull needed further scrutiny, and she made a mental note to write orders for a sedative in order to pry it from the woman's hands.

With that determination made, she began a head-to-toe assessment of the patient. She saw immediately that the woman looked thin and fragile, even though a nasal-gastric tube was supplying her with a solution of food, and an intravenous drip delivered fluids—Sara noted that the IV bag contained 5% dextrose in saline. Whatever ordeal this woman had suffered had left a deep mark, and Sara found herself wondering what had become of the rest of her expedition. But despite the appearance of frailty, the woman was breathing steadily, and showed none of the typical signs of a viral infection. Sara placed an aural thermometer probe in the woman's ear; though not always the most accurate instrument, it was easier to employ when wearing a hazmat suit. The thermometer beeped after a couple seconds and Sara saw that woman's body temperature was actually a degree below normal; no fever, no infection. Sara went down the checklist of possible symptoms, but there was no escaping the simple fact that, aside from being inexplicably unconscious, the woman was healthy.

What did Fulbright know that had prompted him to call in the CDC?

Sara vowed to get to the bottom of that mystery, but she wasn't ready to completely dismiss the idea that the patient had been exposed to something. She methodically drew off thirty ccs of blood from the IV, collected in three separate vials, and placed them in the specimen kit. If the woman had a virus, even one that was presently dormant, there would be evidence of an immune response.

With her work done, Sara left the room. As soon as the door was closed behind her, she doffed the hazmat suit.

Fulbright hastened forward. "Well?"

Sara ignored him and instead addressed Abdullah. "I'd like to get that skull away from her. Just to do some tests on it. Sedate her if you have to."

The Ethiopian doctor frowned, but nodded.

"I don't think there's any risk here," she continued, "but we'll…"

She trailed off as a strange sensation rippled through her. She struggled to interpret the sensory response. It seemed vaguely familiar, and though she couldn't pin it down, she knew it was associated with something bad.

Fulbright picked up on her behavior immediately. "What's wrong?"

His roguish smile had been replaced by something else—grim determination. His expression reminded Sara of Jack Sigler...not as her boyfriend, but as the lethal leader of Chess Team, and that was when she remembered when and where she'd felt this way before.

"Did you hear it? An explosion?"

"I heard nothing," said Abdullah, looking perplexed.

Suddenly, the quiet environment of the hospital ward was shattered by a wailing fire alarm siren.

Fulbright drew a compact semi-automatic pistol from a holster concealed beneath his shirt. "We need to get out of here," he declared. "It's an attack."

Even though she knew better, her first impulse was incredulity. Denial. *It's just a coincidence... He's being paranoid... Everything is going to be okay....*

But the appearance of two men at the end of the hall, dressed head-to-toe in black combat gear and brandishing guns, swept away all trace of doubt.

3.

The taxi rolled three times.

King was sure of that. His perceptions were heightened by the rush of adrenaline through his bloodstream, and everything seemed to be happening in slow motion. Even curled as he was in a protective ball, he watched as the interior of the cab rotated around him, batting him around like a wet sock in a tumble dryer. Each impact was like getting hit by a linebacker in a football game.

But then, after an eternity of spinning and slamming into nearly every surface in the taxi's interior, the cacophony of the Corolla's destruction ceased, and King found himself jammed against the passenger side door, with something heavy pressing down on him.

He lay there for a moment, surprised to still be conscious, grateful to be alive, and vaguely certain that there was something important he should be doing.

Get moving....

Even though the motion had ceased, he felt like his brain was still spinning, flinging his thoughts away before he could string them together in a coherent fashion.

I'm in a taxi, he thought. *There was a rollover accident...*

What's this holding me down?

It was a body; a dead man.

Get moving....

A dead man that got shot by...who again?

It doesn't matter. Someone killed him and they're coming from you. Get moving!

"Get moving, soldier." He said it aloud, like a boot camp drill sergeant, and something inside him clicked. Reaching down past the pain and disorientation, he willed himself to action. He squirmed out from under the weight of the dead driver and took a quick look around.

The taxi had come to rest on its right side. The broken windshield was completely gone, and beyond it he saw the Dodge pick-up that had caused the wreck. It had also rolled, and had come to rest upside-down, only a few feet away. The reinforced roll-cage had prevented anything more serious than cosmetic damage to the vehicle, but the men inside did not appear to have fared as well. King could see the driver through the open window and resting on the inverted headliner. He assumed it was the driver because the man was entangled with the steering column, which had sheared away during the wreck.

King stared at the man, as if in the twisted limbs and blood, he might find some hint of what to do next, and then he remembered; there was a second truck.

The realization galvanized him. He squirmed through the windshield and, propelling himself on elbows and knees, crawled into the overturned Dodge. He scraped past the unmoving—dead?—driver and got a look at the passenger, likewise motionless in a heap on the truck's ceiling. The man still clutched the weapon he had used to strafe the taxi and kill its driver, a Heckler & Koch MP5, fitted with a noise suppressor.

When King tried to wrestle the machine pistol free, the man's eyes fluttered open and he instinctively tried to jerk the gun away. Without a moment's hesitation, King punched the man in the Adam's apple, crushing his trachea. The gun fell from the man's grasp, forgotten, as he commenced clawing at his throat, an activity which occupied him for the last few seconds of his life.

With the MP5 in hand, King wormed through the window opening on the passenger side and onto the hot pavement. He quickly got his feet under him, but stayed low in a crouch, as he peered around the back of the truck's cab. Beyond the wreckage of the taxi, he saw the second truck, parked with both doors open. A man wearing the same digital-camouflage pattern fatigues and tactical gear as the occupants of the crashed truck—and sporting an identical HK MP5—was peering into the smashed taxi.

These guys work in pairs, King thought. He drew back, pivoting on one foot just as the second man rounded the front end of the truck. The gunmen started to bring his weapon up, but King was faster.

The MP5 hardly made any noise at all. The suppressor muffled the report so effectively that King heard only the clicking of the pistol's bolt sliding back and forth, not much louder than a toy gun. Nevertheless, a three-round burst stitched the man's face with blotches of red and he pitched backward.

King was moving before the body hit the ground. He turned again, dropping onto his belly, and low-crawled under the bed of the truck. A cautious peek revealed the remaining gunman crouching at the front of the taxi. The man edged forward and King dropped him with well-aimed burst from the MP5.

King wasted no time. He crawled out from under the pickup and crossed the short distance to where the gunman lay. The fallen man wore a tactical chest rig, similar to the kind Chess Team utilized on mission, with numerous pockets and pouches containing spare magazines, grenades, and other equipment, but there nothing to indicate who he worked for or why he and his comrades had made the assassination attempt. King gathered four magazines for the MP5, then skirted around the front end of the taxi, his weapon at the ready in case he had misjudged the size of the assault force.

He had not. The second truck sat idle, with the front doors open and no one else inside.

Nevertheless, it was too soon to count this as a victory. He had no idea why the men had ambushed him, but it almost certainly had something to do with Sara's assignment, and that meant she was in imminent danger.

Traffic on Ring Road had ground to a halt behind the scene of the accident and curious motorists were disembarking their vehicles to get a better look. Somewhere in the distance, the sound of sirens was audible, and King knew he had to keep moving. He crawled back inside the taxi just long enough to grab his duffel bag then headed for the abandoned pick-up.

The truck was outfitted with a dash-mounted GPS device, and unlike the app for King's phone, this unit communicated directly with the orbiting satellites. He quickly tapped in the coordinates for the hospital, and as the route flashed on the map, he started the engine and sped away from the scene of the ambush.

4.

As he climbed out of the pick-up, King glanced at his watch. Although it felt like hours had passed since he'd left the ambush, according to his Timex, it had been more like ten minutes.

The drive had seemed interminably long. The unfamiliar environment was a flood of new sensory information that had to be interpreted and categorized. At the same time, he wrestled with the mystery of the attack.

His mind was like a computer, sorting what he knew and what he suspected, running through all the possible explanations to see which made the most sense, and like a computer running a complex program, the activity slowed down his processing speed.

He was certain that the four shooters were private contractors, and knew that, once he could establish contact with Deep Blue he'd be able to pin down exactly who they were. The trucks and other equipment would have left a money trail. But because the attackers were in all likelihood hired guns, there was no guarantee that the trail would lead back to the person or organization that had ordered the attack. A connection to Sara's mission in Africa was by no means explicit, but none of the

alternative explanations made any sense.

Dead end, he thought. *I need more information.*

He contemplated calling Deep Blue then and there on the dedicated Chess Team satellite phone stashed in his bag, but he wasn't even sure what questions to ask.

He jogged the half-block from where he'd parked the truck to the hospital's main entrance, his senses on alert for any hint of trouble. The first few steps were excruciating. His body was a mass of bruises from the crash, and as the adrenaline drained away, pain and stiffness had set in with a vengeance. For a few minutes, he moved like the Tin Man from *The Wizard of Oz*, creaky with rust. But he was no stranger to pain. He didn't think he'd suffered any internal injuries, and the muscle soreness would eventually pass. He'd found a first-aid kit in truck, and had used it to clean and bandage the worst of his lacerations, including the wound on his arm where a bullet had grazed him. He had also downed an 800 mg Motrin tablet.

There would be time to rest and heal once he knew that Sara was not in danger.

He entered the hospital building on high alert, his right hand close to the MP5 concealed in the duffel bag slung over his shoulder, but nothing appeared to be amiss. Despite the language barrier, he managed to convey to the woman at the reception desk that he was looking for the CDC team, and a few minutes later, he opened the door to the conference room where the disease detectives had set up a command post.

The room was a hive of activity. Five people—Caucasians all, wearing familiar American clothes—were hastily unpacking computer and laboratory equipment from a stack of plastic containers lined up near the back wall. There was no sign of Sara.

A kindly looking older man noticed him. "Can I help you?"

King frowned. He hadn't anticipated having to deal with Sara's co-workers. The last thing he needed right now was to be

given the runaround. He strode across the room, getting close enough to the man to be able to speak in low voice, barely louder than a whisper. "I need to speak with Dr. Fogg. It's urgent."

The man flashed a patient smile that suggested he was used to hearing people make such claims for the sake of expediency. "I'm Kerry Frey, Dr. Fogg's assistant in charge of personnel. She's busy right now."

"I need to speak with her. I…" He took a deep breath, wondering how much to reveal. "My name is Jack Sigler. She asked me to come here."

A gleam of recognition dawned in the other man's eyes. "So you're Jack. Sara has spoken of you. She's with the patient in the isolation room on the fourth floor…"

Frey's voice trailed off as something else in the room grabbed his attention. King turned, following the direction of the other man's gaze to the door through which he had just entered.

Because he was trained to deal with surprises, King did not lapse into the same paralysis that now afflicted Frey, but he was nevertheless taken aback by the pair of figures, all in black from the soles of their combat boots to the tops of the balaclavas which almost completely covered their faces. A curse formed on his lips, but before he could speak the word, the two figures, in perfect synchronization, each tossed something into the room.

"Shit!"

Even though the objects were tumbling through the air, King recognized them immediately. Black metal tubes about three inches long, an inch in diameter, and perforated with a Swiss cheese pattern of holes.

Flash-bangs! Shit!

There was no time to seek cover, no time to even shout a warning. King did the only thing he could think of: he dropped to the floor, curling up like a hedgehog. He pressed his face into his thighs, and covered his ears with his forearms.

Suddenly, the world was transformed into pure light and noise. It was like being inside a lightning bolt. The flash of the magnesium/ammonium nitrate pyrotechnic charge in the M84 stun grenade lit up every fiber of King's body; even with his eyes covered, he "saw" the flare as a red-yellow blaze. Simultaneously, the detonation produced a wave of sound that drove through his head like a freight train.

But King had been trained to deal with the after-effects of a flash-bang; he knew how to cope with the disorientation of sensory overload, and more importantly, knew the consequences of not taking immediate defensive action.

When he opened his eyes, the room seemed dark, as if all the lights had been switched off, but King could see two shapes moving through the room. One of the figures stopped and a tongue of flame erupted from his outstretched arm. Even through the ringing in his ears, King could hear the sound of gunfire.

His hand found the grip of his MP5 and he triggered a burst in the direction of the nearest gunmen. The shots hit center-mass, driving the man back a few steps but he didn't go down.

Body armor. Shit, shit, shit!

King got his feet under him and scrambled to the back of the room. He could just make out the chest-high stack of equipment crates, and while he knew they probably wouldn't stop a bullet, they would at least afford him a degree of concealment. He crouched low, scanning both angles of approach, and waited for the killers to make their move.

The attack didn't come.

His vision and hearing were both returning by degrees, but neither sense gave him any hint of what was happening on the other side of stacked containers. No more shots were fired, and if the gunmen were speaking to each other, their voices were too soft for him to discern. Shouldering the MP5, he rose out of his crouch for just an instant, and peered over the top of the barrier.

The shooters were gone. King cautiously emerged from concealment, sweeping the room with the barrel of his machine pistol, but his first assessment was correct; the assault force had finished their grisly task and fallen back. King was alone with the dead.

He spied the unmoving form of the older man he had first spoken with. A ragged hole had been torn in his chest, almost certainly the result of a several bullets in a tight grouping.

Kerry Frey, he thought. *He had a name. He probably had a family and friends. He worked with Sara....*

Sara!

King started for the exit, but before he could cross half the distance, he saw another pair grenades sail through the air in the room. Not flash-bangs this time, but cylinders—like stubby aerosol cans—gray in color, marked with purple bands.

Incendiary grenades.

Shit.

5.

Fulbright thrust Sara behind him and then snapped off a couple shots in the direction of the masked gunmen. Despite openly wielding firearms, the men seemed caught off guard. They fell back, out of view and did not reappear for several seconds. Fulbright, on the other hand, had reacted almost without thinking.

He expected this, Sara thought. *He knew this attack was coming.*

But there was no time to give voice to her suspicions. The man she suspected of being a CIA officer gripped her arm and all but dragged her away from the gunmen and, she hoped, toward safety. She looked over her shoulder and saw the two doctors seemingly paralyzed by the unexpected violence, and then they were lost from view as Fulbright pulled her through a doorway into a stairwell which was already crowded with people evacuating in response to the fire alarm.

Sara immediately turned toward the descending flight, but an insistent tug on her arm drew her in the other direction. Up.

"My team."

Fulbright's voice, like his expression, was grim. "What do you think that explosion was? If your team is still alive, there's nothing we can do to help them. I need to get you out of here."

Still alive? If? Sara shook her head. It couldn't be true. It just couldn't.

As they climbed the stairs, pushing through the fleeing horde, Fulbright took a phone from his shirt pocket and made a call. "It's me. Things have gone to shit here. I need air evac, ASAP." Then, in a tone dripping with sarcasm, he added: "Five minutes ago would be nice."

As the phone disappeared back into his pocket, Sara managed to get out a question. "What the hell is going on?"

Fulbright glanced back at her, his face stony and determined. His expression made her think of Jack; she desperately wished that he was the one leading her confidently through this crisis. She half expected Fulbright to dismiss the inquiry, but he surprised her. "That woman was exposed to something—some kind of pathogen. Something that can be made into a weapon."

The information stimulated the analytical part of her brain, and for a moment, thoughts of grief and concern for her own safety were relegated to secondary priority. "Why didn't you tell me any of this? We could have had security in place to prevent this. Hell, we should have airlifted her back to Atlanta."

"I didn't expect this." Fulbright's tone was self-effacing. "I should have, but I didn't think they'd try anything like this."

She didn't know whether to believe him, but that wasn't the important question. "Who are they?"

Fulbright turned his gaze forward, steering her around another landing—the eighth floor—and kept climbing. The flow of people responding to the fire alarm had dried up; evidently, everyone on the uppermost floors had already exited. "I think it's Nexus Genetics, the company Felice Carter works for. They sent her out there to find something like this, prehistoric genetic material, an ancient virus. But something went wrong. The expedition must have been exposed to something. That's all I know really."

"You think they found what they were looking for?"

"I wasn't sure. Now I am. The answer is in those samples you took. We have to protect them." He looked back at her again. "I have to protect you. And you have to figure out just what it is they found, and come up with some kind of vaccine."

Sara nodded. "That's what I do. But I need my team. My equipment."

"Once you're safe, I'll get you what you need." He took a breath, and then added. "We'll find a way to contact your team."

If they're still alive. Fulbright didn't say it. He didn't need to.

The stairs ended on a landing blocked by a heavy metal door. Fuller cautiously pushed the door open and peered out. Sara looked over his shoulder and saw a helicopter sitting idle on the rooftop, about a hundred meters away.

"That was fast," she said.

But Fulbright pushed her back and pulled the door shut. "That's not our ride."

In the silence that followed, Sara's hypersensitive ears detected the sound of footsteps echoing up the stairwell—judging by the cadence, there were at least three different people—and she didn't have to ask who the helicopter did belong to.

Fulbright was taking out his phone, preparing to make another call, but she gripped his arm, forestalling him. "They're coming."

6.

The Old Mother dreamed of a place of death.

"Old Mother" was what her clan called her. The honorific was a sign of great respect; her stature in the clan was something akin to what would, many thousands of years hence, be called 'divine.'

Indeed, it was she who had brought forth the great change, though few in the clan truly understood just how important that was. Only two of her children still lived and could recall the time before, when their fathers had been no different than the other beasts living in the valley, unable to make or understand speech, able to use only the crudest of tools, fearful of fire despite the Old Mother's mastery of the element. She alone remembered what it had been like before that.

Her earliest recollections were of frustration. Her head was filled with thoughts which she yearned to share, but the grunts which the others in the clan used to communicate could not convey such complicated things. Worse still, the others seemed incapable of sharing her sense of wonder at the world that surrounded them. She had been thrilled by her discovery, as a very young child, that it was possible to use the sharp edges of a broken rock to cut through animal flesh, but when she had tried to show the dominant male, he had cuffed her in the head and taken the fresh kill for himself.

Yet, although she had been an outsider even among her own kind, her unique gifts served her well. The dominant male had taken her as his mate, protecting and feeding her, while other females were allowed to perish when food was scarce, and in time, when she bore offspring, she discovered that they shared her abilities. She conceived of a way to pass information to them, a system of communication where sounds and gestures had specific meaning that all of them understood.

Not surprisingly, her children thrived. Her first male child matured to become the dominant male, and his offspring, as well as all those of the Old Mother's brood, also shared her gift. Within two generations, all the offspring born to the clan were of her bloodline.

Now she was old. It had been a long time since the blood flowed from her loins, even longer since any of the males showed even the slightest desire to mate with her. In many ways, her offspring had surpassed her, building on the knowledge she had given to them, innovating, and improving their common language to express new concepts and make new discoveries.

But she was still the Old Mother, and greatly honored.

And she was the only one who had the dreams.

The dreams guided the clan, leading them to abundant hunting grounds, guiding them to water and shelter, warning of dangers like the coming of storms that took fire from the sky and set the grasslands ablaze. She had taught the others how to read signs in earth and sky—to anticipate the changing of the seasons, or the migration of the animals—but none of her children or her children's children experienced the visions that first enabled her to grasp these concepts. When she was gone, the dreams would be no more.

That time was drawing near. This also she had dreamed.

She dreamed of a place of death. She dreamed of her destiny approaching like a great gray wall, emerging from the setting sun.

Then, one night, she awoke from the dream.

It was time.

The Old Mother looked around the cave where the clan slept, oblivious to their wondrous future. The dim embers of the cook-fire offered little illumination, but she could make out the clumped shapes of mated pairs and families huddled together in repose.

She struggled to her feet, her age clinging to her withering muscles and creaky joints. It was good that this moment had finally come; in a few more turnings of the moon, she wouldn't be able to move at all.

None in the clan stirred as she made her way to the mouth of the cave. A half-moon cast a silvery glow on the landscape and a bright river of stars lit up the sky. Yet, the Old Mother did not need illumination; the path she followed was one glimpsed in a dream and she could have followed it blind.

She walked all night, the urgency of her purpose pushing her onward through the pain and fatigue. At last, as the sun broke over the horizon, she found them.

She was not unfamiliar with the great beasts. The land belonged to them. Like her clan, they were herd animals, usually gathering in groups that numbered more than she could count on all of her fingers. From time to time, the clan would hunt them, taking stragglers that were too old or weak to keep up with the herd, but there was great risk in that endeavor. Even the weakest of the great beasts could crush them with hardly a second thought. The clan never approached a herd directly.

This herd was like nothing she had ever seen before.

Their numbers were, despite her gift, beyond her ability to comprehend. They were a great mass, stretching out in the direction where the sun would set at day's end, farther than her eye could see. And as she drew near, they began to stir.

A shiver of excitement gripped her as the beasts began trumpeting and stamping their massive feet. She was afraid and awestruck, but this was the moment she had dreamed of, and witnessing the great herd, feeling the earth shake as they danced, was strangely satisfying.

Then, from out of the thunderous mass, several of the beasts advanced.

They were old, like her, the matriarchs of dozens of herds. She felt a tremor of fear as they drew close, surrounding her, but they did not attack. Instead, acting in unison, they knelt before her.

Images flooded into her mind, the thoughts not just of the matriarchs, but of the entire assembly, and a scream tore from her throat....

Δ Δ Δ

Felice Carter awoke from her long dream, and opened her eyes in the middle of a nightmare.

7.

King spun away an instant before the thermate compound in each grenade ignited. Unlike the flash-bangs, there was no detonation, no deafening blast. Rather, there was only a flare of light, as bright as an arc welder, followed by a palpable wave of heat that permeated the room.

The carpeted floor instantly erupted in flames, as did the wooden tables nearest the ignition. The molded plastic containers which had been used to transport the CDC team's equipment began to melt, despite being several feet away from the flames, and as the emerging conflagration began to destroy natural fibers and manmade compounds alike, a miasma of black smoke filled the room.

All of this happened in mere seconds.

King felt the waves of heat at his back and the stinging of chemical fumes in his eyes as he searched the room for some other exit. He couldn't exit through the door; the gunmen would almost certainly be waiting for him. What did that leave?

Through the persistent ringing in his ears he heard a new sound, the low wailing of a fire alarm, and at almost the same instant, it started to rain in the room. King glanced back, trying to avoid directly looking at the blinding incendiary flares, and saw that the automated sprinkler system was having little effect on the fire. The droplets simply flashed to steam, while under the shelter of the tables, the flames were spreading.

He returned his attention to the matter of escaping the room. There were no windows, but as his vision improved, he saw that one of the walls was different. It was not a true wall, but rather a series of temporary partitions that had been set up to divide a much larger area into two smaller rooms. He dashed past the blossoming inferno to the partition, stepped back and then delivered his best door-smashing kick.

The partition didn't budge. His heel rebounded and a wave of agony shuddered through his entire body, aggravating injuries that he didn't even know he'd suffered. A grunt of pain escaped through his clenched teeth.

Stupid, Jack. Very stupid.

He shook off the hurt and took another look at the partition. It was mounted on tracks, one on the floor and another on the ceiling, similar to a sliding patio door, and secured in place with a flush-bolt. He thumbed the latch mechanism and heard a click as the bolt released, allowing him to slide the partition away with almost no effort.

Lesson learned, he thought. *Think next time.*

He sprinted through the adjoining room to the door in the corner, and with his MP5 ready, pushed it open.

Beyond was a scene of total chaos as people fled in response to the fire alarm. He peeked out, looking down the hallway, and saw two black-clad figures lingering at the doorway to the other half of the conference room, a good thirty meters away. Their very presence only intensified the general hysteria, but they seemed oblivious; their attention was fixed on the doorway.

He considered taking them out but quickly dismissed the idea. He knew they were wearing body armor, so the only way to guarantee a kill was a head shot. He might be able to get one of them, but if he failed to get them both, it would mean a firefight, and that would only keep him from his real objective, to say nothing of putting a lot of innocent lives in jeopardy.

He took a deep breath, and then strode out into the hall-way, moving into the crowd of people evacuating from deeper within the hospital. The urge to look back at the gunmen was almost overwhelming, but doing so would risk drawing their attention. Instead, he focused on searching the crowd for Sara. She wasn't there, but as he moved through their midst, he soon located a stairwell packed with people escaping the upper levels. Like a salmon thrashing up the face of a waterfall, he muscled into the mass of people and started climbing.

He recalled what Frey had told him, just before the attack. Sara had gone to the fourth floor. Was she still there?

Is she still alive?

King abandoned all pretense of being polite. We waved the gun ahead of him, and the crowd parted like sea in some biblical miracle. He reached the fourth floor a few moments later and burst through the door.

Most visitors had already evacuated, but the medical staff was busy moving patients, beds and all, to the elevator. Hospitals were one of the few places where using elevators in a fire was an absolute necessity. King caught the eye of one of the nurses, and was about to ask for Sara's whereabouts, when a bloodcurdling shriek from down the hall startled them both.

"Never mind," King breathed, and took off in the direction of the noise.

It wasn't Sara. That wasn't just wishful thinking. It hadn't been Sara's voice—he knew that with complete certainty—but more to the point, he couldn't imagine any circumstances where Sara would scream. That knowledge however didn't necessarily make him feel any better. Whatever was causing the persistent howl couldn't be good.

The shriek led him to an open door, and he charged through with the MP5 at the ready. The scream was issuing from the woman thrashing in the single hospital bed in the room, but King barely noticed her. His attention was fixed on the two men in black assault gear that stood on the far side of the bed. One of them was in the process of sealing a plastic biohazard bag over what looked to King like a skull. The other was raising his gun.

King shot him between the eyes, but even as his finger released the trigger, the full impact of what he had just seen landed on him like a ton of bricks. *That gun....*

He shifted the machine pistol to the left, ready to take out the other attacker, but withheld fire when he saw the incendiary grenade in the man's outstretched right hand. The pin was out and only the pressure of his fingers, covering the trigger spoon, kept it from deflagrating.

"Kill me and we all burn," snarled the gunman.

King kept the weapon trained on the man and weighed the consequences of simply taking the shot. He knew he could escape the room before the grenade started burning, but there were other considerations, not the least of which was the hysterical patient.

The shooter edged away from the bed, the biohazard bag with its mysterious contents tucked under his left arm. He glanced down at his fallen comrade, and then met King's stare. Although the balaclava concealed his visage, there was no mistaking the rage burning in his eyes. "Maybe not today, but you're a dead man."

King ignored the bluster, keeping his gaze and his MP5 steady as the man backed toward the door, but both of them knew exactly how it would end. The man took one more step toward the door, and then threw the grenade.

The gray cylinder arced through the air and landed on the bed. King squeezed the trigger, but the man was already gone, ducking as he fled into the hallway. The shot was an indulgence—a Hail Mary pass—and he hadn't really expected to hit his target. Hit or miss, he had other things to worry about.

Unlike standard fragmentation grenades, which had a 3-to-5

second time delay fuze, the M201A1 igniter in the incendiary grenade burned in less than 2 seconds. In the instant he saw the spoon fly away from grenade body, even before it left his opponent's hand, King started a very short countdown clock.

One Mississippi....

Even as the grenade landed on the bed... even as the round from his MP5 flashed through the suppressor on its way to nowhere, King's mind tumbled with conflicting priorities.

The grenade! Deal with that first. How?

Two Mississippi....

He must have been counting too fast because nothing had happened yet.

None too gently, he snared the female patient's flailing arm with his left hand and pulled her to him. In the same motion, he launched a kick at the bed's side rail. Because its roll-brake had been engaged, the heavy bed only scooted a couple yards. Before King could lower his extended foot, the room was filled with brilliant white light.

He looked away quickly, but bright streaks now painted his retinas. The bed erupted in flames and smoke, both rendered almost invisible by the intensely bright fire from the burning grenade. Barely able to see anything except with his peripheral vision, King knelt over the frantic woman, hugging her to his chest, and stabbed the MP5 at the doorway.

He figured the odds were about fifty-fifty that the black clad intruder would be waiting for him in the hall; he expected to walk into a blast from the man's very distinctive handgun. But staying in the room was not an option, and 'maybe dead' beat 'definitely dead' any day of the week.

This time, the odds broke in his favor. The other man was gone, evidently eager to escape with the prize contained in the plastic biohazard bag.

"You can let go."

The voice, weak and breathless, startled him. He glanced down at the woman, locked in the embrace of his left arm, and realized she was no longer thrashing. He eased the pressure of his grip, but didn't release her. She didn't look strong enough to stand on her own, much less negotiate four flights of stairs to safety. Despite her abruptly calm demeanor, there was a trace of madness in her eyes. Her face was streaked with something that looked like baby food, and blood was leaking from her arm where her IV had ripped out.

King glanced at the blood, and for the first time, it occurred to him that this woman was almost certainly the patient whom Kerry Frey had spoken of, the patient in the isolation room. The patient whose illness had summoned Sara and her team across the ocean in the first place.

Wonderful, he thought, trying to imagine what almost-always-fatal new disease he had just been exposed to. There were definite drawbacks to having a CDC disease detective for a girlfriend.

But Sara wasn't here. He didn't think she would have abandoned a patient when the fire alarm sounded. So where was she?

Black smoke was beginning to billow from the open doorway, and he felt the glow of radiant heat on the exposed skin of his face and arms.

He turned to the woman again. "What's your name?"

"Felice."

"Felice, I'm Jack. I'm going to get you out of here, but you need to do what I say, okay?"

She nodded.

"Can you walk?"

"I think so. Let go." He did, gradually releasing his embrace, but ready to catch her if her strength failed. After a few seconds on her own, she nodded again. "I can manage."

"Good. Then let's get the hell out of here."

8.

Fulbright cocked his head sideways, listening, and then frowned as he too heard the sound of footsteps echoing up the stairwell. "Damn it. All right, this isn't going to be pretty. Just stay close to me."

The lady or the tiger? Sara thought, recalling the classic short story of a Roman gladiator faced with two equally undesirable choices. She half-expected him to charge down the stairs, headlong into the force of unknown but surely superior strength, with guns blazing in typical CIA cowboy fashion, but instead he chose the other door. Literally.

He opened the roof access door just enough for them to squeeze through single file. As she stepped out, Sara got a better look at the waiting helicopter, and at the two men who appeared to be guarding it. Like the pair she had seen in hospital ward, they were clad entirely in black assault gear.

Sara felt very exposed as she followed Fulbright along the perimeter of the raised concrete superstructure that housed the stairwell. She expected at any moment to hear gunfire. Or maybe she wouldn't hear anything; the bullet that would snuff her out of existence would probably be traveling faster than the sound of the shot.

That's the kind of thing Jack would know.

But if the two men noticed their presence, they gave no indication.

Suddenly, the roof access door flew open behind them with such force that it rebounded off the exterior wall with a bang that, given Sara's state of mind, sounded like a shot. She whirled involuntarily and caught sight of a lone individual, dressed in the now familiar black uniform, sprinting toward the helicopter. As he passed them, Sara saw that he was carrying a clear plastic bag with a large white-yellow object inside.

The ape skull!

The man did not even glance in their direction, but a moment later, two more men burst from the door, and they did look.

Sara gaped at them. It was like watching a movie. The two men turned, squared their shoulders, and raised their guns.

Fulbright grabbed her arm and propelled her past him. "Go!"

He fired several shots in the direction of the two gunmen. One of them winced but shrugged the impact off as though it were nothing more than a slap. Then, their guns spoke.

The report was thunderous, far louder than Fulbright's pistol. Concrete exploded above Sara's head, showering her with grit, but then she rounded the corner with Fulbright right behind her.

"Keep going," he shouted.

Sara ran, but no more shots were fired. Instead, she heard the whine of the helicopter's turbines powering up. In a matter of seconds, the whoosh of the rotor blades carving the air became audible and quickened to a roar of engine noise and wind.

They rounded the corner to the back side of the superstructure where Fulbright signaled for her to stop. He ejected the magazine from his pistol, reloaded, and then began scanning in both directions for signs of pursuit. Sara cocked her head, hoping to hear the sound of footsteps, but the noise of the helicopter drowned out everything.

It became apparent after a few minutes that the gunmen weren't going to engage them. Sara heard the change in pitch as the helicopter lifted off and then flew almost horizontally away from the rooftop. Fulbright edged around the corner as the tempest quieted.

"They're gone."

Sara sagged against the wall, but her relief quickly gave way to anger. "All right. Answers."

Fulbright's face was flushed with the exertions of running and fighting, but he tried to bring back his roguish smile. "I told you everything I know."

"Like hell you did. You know a lot more than you're letting on. Your secrets put me and my team…" She faltered as she recalled Fulbright's earlier comment. Her co-workers—her friends—might already be dead. "If something has happened to them, it's on your head."

Fulbright sighed, his expression contrite. "I knew there was some risk. People who try to develop bio-weapons usually don't have a lot of scruples. But I couldn't have known anyone would try something like this."

His words did nothing to soothe her, but she saw that there was nothing to be gained by venting her rage. She took a deep breath and tried to focus on the bigger picture. "What do you know about this pathogen they're after? That woman—Dr. Carter—she didn't look sick. I don't think she was sick."

He spread his hands. "I told you what they were looking for—some kind of ancient virus. When Felice Carter came back from the expedition, in the state you saw her in, I assumed that she had become infected. That's why I sent for you. And the fact that somebody hit us here today, tells me that I was right. She found something out there and brought it back."

"It didn't look like that assault team was interested in her. But they took that ape skull she was holding."

"They did?" Fulbright's forehead creased in a frown. "Damn it. I should have realized how important that was."

"Maybe it doesn't matter. Even if there is useful genetic material in that skull, it's very unlikely that it's going to turn out to be some kind of super monkey flu. And if there is something like that, Dr. Carter would have been exposed to it and there will be evidence in the blood samples I took." She pushed away from the wall. "I need to get back down to my team. I have to know that they're okay."

Before Fulbright could answer, his phone chirped. He took it out and glanced at the caller ID before answering. "What's your ETA?...Good, we're on the roof." He covered the phone with a hand and addressed Sara. "They wouldn't have hit us here if they weren't certain that Felice had what they were looking for."

He uncovered the phone. "Send a ground team here to collect the rest of the CDC team and their equipment. Take them to the safe house."

He thumbed the end button and turned to Sara again. His face was stony with resolve. "Our ride will be here in two minutes. Those blood samples just became the most important thing in the world. I have to keep them, and you, safe."

9.

A firefighter spied King and Felice as they left the stairwell on the first floor, and guided them to the exit. The fire in the conference room appeared to have been contained, but a pall of smoke hung in the air and the damage appeared considerable.

Outside, King scanned the crowd. There were a few white faces among the dark-skinned local population, but no sign of Sara. He heard the distinctive sound of a helicopter taking off from the roof, high overhead; it could only be the assault force making their getaway.

"We're exposed here," he told Felice. It was perhaps a poor choice of words. In her hospital gown, Felice was very literally exposed. Fortunately, there were dozens of other patients in a similar state of undress filling the street in front of the hospital, and no one seemed to notice her. King however wasn't worried about someone ogling her.

The men in Felice's room had been armed with a very distinctive type of pistol. Normally, when staring down the barrel of a gun, a person doesn't try to identify the make and model, but the Metal Storm O'Dwyer VLe pistols the men had been wielding sported a unique four-barrel configuration that was impossible not to recognize. The VLe pistols were radically different from traditional guns in that they had no moving parts. Instead of a mechanism to advance one round at a time into the firing chamber, the Metal Storm pistol had caseless rounds already stacked in its four barrels, and fired them with an electrical charge. A single trigger pull could unload the pistol in a fraction of a second. The design was still considered experimental, and prototypes were prohibitively expensive for the run-of-the-mill mercenary.

"I think those men planned to kill you," he continued, "and there's a good chance some of them stayed behind to make sure the job was done."

"Kill me?" It was clearly too much for her to process.

"Just stay close to me. We'll sort this out when we get somewhere safe." King knew of only one group that used Metal Storm pistols. And if that was who wanted Felice dead, that was all the reason King needed to protect her.

As they moved toward the edge of the throng, King dug out his Chess Team phone. He was just about to make a call when a young Ethiopian man stepped in front of him

"You look like you need some help," he said in perfect, albeit slightly accented English.

King regarded the newcomer with suspicion, and when he put the phone back in his bag, his hand found the grip of the MP5, which he had stashed just before leaving the stairwell. "Thanks friend, but I think we can manage."

The Ethiopian smiled, but edged closer and lowered his voice to a surreptitious whisper. "I saw what happened. I know they came for her. I can help you."

King shook his head. "If you know that, then you know why I'm not exactly eager to trust you."

"You should." The young man turned to Felice. "You know me, don't you?"

Felice looked at him then raised her eyes to King, showing no hint of recognition.

The man's smile slipped a notch, as if disappointed by her

failure to remember him. "I'm Moses—Moses Selassie. I was with you on the expedition to the Rift Valley. I rescued you from the cave—"

Felice's eyes grew wide and she grabbed Moses by the shoulders. "The cave? You must take me back."

>>>Report.

Where should I start? It was a disaster. The CDC team is dead, except for Fogg. And my men failed to get Sigler. He took out the entire assault force. Four men. He's in the wind now. Who the hell is this guy?

>>>Data concerning Sigler's current activities are classified at the highest level. The probability that he is part of a clandestine military or counter-intelligence agency has increased to 92.3%. There is insufficient information to determine what his most probable next course of action will be.

Like I need you to tell me that.

>>>Do you believe Sigler will attempt to establish contact with Fogg?

I would if I were him.

>>>That must not be permitted.

I got it covered.

10.

It wasn't until they were settled in Moses' tenement on the edge of the city, that King realized Felice wasn't Ethiopian. She hadn't spoken more than a few words, and he'd been a little too busy trying to keep her alive to pay attention to the fact that she didn't speak with an accent. When their host had stepped out to purchase food and some clothes to replace her hospital garment, she had remained withdrawn, and King had been content to leave her alone a little while longer.

He felt as though he had been handed the pieces of a jig-saw puzzle, minus the box with a picture of what it would look like when correctly assembled. He had a stack of clues, but no idea how they related to each other. But it was his uncertainty about Sara's fate that consumed his thoughts.

They hit the CDC team first. That wasn't an accident. But Sara wasn't in Felice's room. She missed them. And somehow I missed her. So where is she now? Are they still looking for her?

Moses returned after about an hour, carrying several loaves of *injera*, a local sourdough flatbread, and a container of *wat*, a spicy beef stew. He also presented Felice with a traditional garment. She examined it with obvious disdain.

"It is the *habesha qemis*," he explained. "The dress worn for the coffee ceremony. Many women wear them."

"We can go out later and get you whatever you want," King said. "Unless you really prefer that hospital gown."

She sighed. "Looks like I'm going native. Turn around boys; give a girl a little privacy."

King complied. "West coast, right?"

"Kirkland, Washington."

"So what brings you to Africa? What's your story?"

There was a long silence, then: "You can turn around now."

The coffee dress was not exactly flattering, but it was an improvement. Moses smiled approvingly then set about preparing a meal, while King repeated his question.

"You mean you don't already know?"

King regarded her for a moment, and then folded his arms over his chest. "Okay. Cards on the table. I'll show you mine, you show me yours. Here's what I know.

"Yesterday, a CDC team was scrambled out of Atlanta to investigate a possible outbreak, here in Ethiopia. Patient zero— the person suspected of being the source of the outbreak—is you. He—" King gestured at Moses—"talked about an expedition and a cave, which answers a few questions, but raises a hell of a lot more."

He noticed her squirm at the mention of the cave.

"But I'll get to that in a minute. About fifteen minutes after the CDC team arrived, they were all dead. The guys who killed them then proceeded to your room where they almost took you out as well. So, that's what I 'already know.' Now, it's your turn. I'm going to ask this one more time, as diplomatically as I know how." He paused for effect, and when he spoke again, he enunciated each word as if driving nails with a hammer. "What the fuck is going on?"

She winced at his tone, but then straightened, as if drawing on some previously untapped vein of courage. "I guess I owe you that much.

"I was part of an expedition to the Great Rift Valley, in northern Ethiopia. I'm a geneticist, but I specialize in paleobiology. One of the things my company does is investigate the historical record, including more esoteric sources—myths and folklore—in order to secure previously undiscovered sources of genetic material. Our information led to the discovery of a cave in the Afar Region."

He sensed there was a lot more to that part of the story, but didn't press her. "Then what?"

"Then…I don't know. We found the cave, but I don't remember anything after that. Nothing until the hospital." She nodded to Moses. "Ask him."

King turned his gaze to their host who was in the process of ladling portions of stew onto pieces of flatbread, using the latter like serving plates. He put the food in front of each of them, and then sat down. "I can only tell you what I saw. I was just a laborer, hired to help set up the camp outside the cave."

"You're very well spoken for a laborer."

"Being able to speak your language certainly helped me get the job. But I assure you, I was nothing more than a common bearer." He made a sweeping gesture. "Look around. I am a man of humble means. I take whatever work I can find."

"Go on."

"For many days, everything went well. But then, the researchers in the cave stopped coming out. Three days passed with no word. There was a great deal of unrest in the camp. Some of the men started a riot. In the confusion, I went into the cave and found you." He nodded to Felice. "You were unconscious, so I carried you out. I found a truck and drove you back to the city."

"And you've been hanging around the hospital ever since?" King asked.

Moses shrugged, still looking at Felice. "I was concerned about you, but I dared not come forward. You see, the expedition...the camp was completely destroyed. The police would not have believed my account of events, so after I dropped you off anonymously, I kept checking to see if you had regained consciousness. I had hoped you would be able to verify my account of what happened."

King waved his hand emphatically. "Back up. We're glossing over the important part here. What happened in that cave during those three days?"

Moses and Felice looked to each other, but neither had an answer.

King pointed to the woman first. "You were in there. You found something, right? Found whatever it is you were looking for? Those men that attacked us today took something from you. It looked like a skull. Do you remember that?"

Felice appeared troubled by the question, but shook her head. Moses however spoke up. "Yes, you had an ape skull in the cave. When I brought you out, you were clinging to it. You would not let me take it out of your hands."

"Okay, let's put a pin in that. Now, there were other researchers in that cave, right? What happened to them?" When he got no answer, King persisted. "Come on. The CDC was called in. Somebody thinks you found a virus or something. Did you? Did they all get sick and die in there? Is that why you were unconscious?"

"I am not ill," Moses offered. "I entered the cave and spent two days in contact with her, yet I have not shown any signs of infection."

"Okay, so not a virus. But something, right? Something to do with that skull?" Blank looks. King realized he wasn't going to get anything more out of them, so he switched gears again. "Felice, who do you work for?"

"A company called Nexus Genetics. They're based in Seattle."

Nexus? That wasn't the answer he had been expecting. "How long have you been with them?"

"From the beginning. A little over two years now. They were formed when my old company was broken up."

"Let me guess. Manifold Genetics."

"You've heard of us?"

With no little effort, King controlled his expression. "The team that hit the hospital was Gen-Y, Manifold's private security army. They were tying up loose ends."

Felice's eyes widened in sincere alarm. King knew from experience that, even though Manifold's founder, Richard Ridley, was quite literally a monster, many of the scientists he had employed were innocent pawns in his quest for power. Some of them, and even a few Gen-Y personnel, had been instrumental in bringing Manifold down. But Ridley had survived and gone underground, and it seemed that Manifold had as well. And though Ridley was now believed to be dead, it appeared his directives were still being carried out. There was another option, though. One that King hoped wasn't at play. Before his death, Ridley uncovered an ancient language—the original language, or Mother Tongue, which was capable of affecting the physical world in profound ways best described as Biblical—light from darkness, life granted to the inanimate, physical healing. Before being subdued, he used the language to create several duplicates of himself. Many of the duplicates were destroyed, but there was no way to know how many he created or how many of them still operated around the world. That Nexus Genetics, which had, he surmised, been cobbled together from some of the pieces of Manifold, still carried out Ridley's agenda was an ominous sign.

There will still pieces that didn't quite fit, but King was starting to see the picture now. It was time to call Deep Blue. "You're safe now," he told her as he got out his Chess Team phone. "I'll arrange transport back to the States."

"No." Felice's voice was edged with panic.

King lowered the phone. "No?"

"I need to go back to the cave." She turned to Moses. "You can take me there. You remember the way?"

Moses nodded uncertainly, but then looked to King, as if for reassurance.

"You said they were 'tying up loose ends,' right?" Felice continued. "They'll be going after the cave next. You know I'm right. We have to get there first."

"You don't even remember what you found."

"No, I don't. But somehow I just know that I have to go back there."

King frowned. This wasn't what he needed right now. Sara was still out there somewhere, probably in grave danger. But Felice was right about the cave being a loose end. And if it was the source of whatever discovery had prompted the attack on the hospital, then getting there ahead of a Gen-Y clean-up crew was imperative. Where Ridley and Manifold were concerned, immediate action was required.

He turned to Moses. "Think you can put together an expedition? Get us outfitted with supplies? Discreetly?"

"It will be costly."

King loosened his belt to reveal a concealed zipper pouch, and from it he took a stack of coins which he pressed into the Ethiopian's hand. The weight of ten solid gold Krugerrands caught Moses off guard and his fist almost fell into what was left of his meal.

King gave a tight smile. "I think that should cover it."

11.

As soon as they arrived at Fulbright's "safe house," Sara transferred the blood samples from her bag to the refrigerator. Less than an hour had passed since she and Fulbright had been whisked away from the hospital by helicopter. A short flight to a private airfield had followed, and almost immediately upon arriving, they had driven to a house in an upscale neighborhood in Bole, south of the city.

Sara felt like a piece of driftwood in a raging river. Caught in the current of events beyond her control, there was not even the illusion of choice. She clutched the specimen bag like a lifeline; at least that was something she understood. She had to keep the blood drawn from Felice Carter viable. Processing the specimens and learning what secrets they held would have to wait until the team showed up with the equipment.

That was what she kept telling herself.

But as she watched Fulbright's face change during yet another phone conversation, she knew that wasn't going to happen. When he finally rang off and turned to her, she quickly sat down.

"The fire started in the lab," he said in a quiet voice. "They recovered five bodies, all badly burned. It wasn't an accident.

The police aren't saying anything more, but there's going to be an investigation."

Sara closed her eyes and took a breath. She knew she should be shocked or sad, but she just couldn't wrap her head around it. She had only left Frey and the others for a few minutes to assess the patient, and part of her believed that they were still there, waiting for her to return. It was almost too much to comprehend that they had all been ripped out of the world. She took another deep breath. "I have to make contact with CDC headquarters. I have to let them know what's happened."

Fulbright pursed his lips. "I don't think that's a good idea. Whoever did this, they specifically targeted your team. They knew you were coming and they wanted to make sure you couldn't get the job done. By now, they've probably had time to figure out that they didn't complete that job, and that means they'll be looking for you. We have to keep you off the radar."

"I can't do anything without equipment."

Fulbright nodded. "We can order whatever you need and have it overnighted."

"We're talking very specialized equipment. Thousands of dollars. And I'll still have to be able to uplink with the CDC in order to make sense of whatever I discover."

"Money isn't an issue. Right now, I'm more concerned with figuring out who's behind this."

A concealed vault door, equipped with both a numeric lock and a retinal scanning device, led to an austere computer room. Fulbright logged onto a desktop terminal and then, with Sara's guidance, started ordering medical equipment from private sector supply companies. Sara kept her shopping list modest, and after about an hour had put together a field expedient research lab. Fulbright produced a platinum American Express card and paid for it all, as well as the hefty overnight shipping charges, without a second look.

"There's nothing more you can do right now," Fulbright

told her when they had concluded. "You should get some rest. Maybe something to eat."

She nodded perfunctorily. While they had been occupied with procuring the equipment, she had been able to cope, but now a wave of fatigue and loss was looming. The only way to stave off a crash was to keep busy, keep her mind engaged with the problem.

"Listen," she said, pausing at the doorway. "I know somebody who might be able to help us sort this out. He has access to resources that…" She left the sentence hanging; if Fulbright was what she thought he was, he would understand.

And he seemed to. He regarded her thoughtfully. "This friend of yours…He works for the government, right?"

He leaned back in his chair and sighed. "I'm guessing you know a little something about interdepartmental rivalries. Sometimes agencies work against each other, usually unintentionally, and the left hand doesn't know what the right is doing."

"What's your point?"

"Until I have a better idea who is behind all this, I really don't know who to trust. This could have been an op sanctioned by another agency. We can't trust anyone right now."

Sara felt a flare of indignation. "Jack would never be involved in something like that."

"I'm sure you're right. But if we reach out to him, we might send up a red flag. Someone will put two and two together and compromise us." Before she could protest again, his demeanor softened. "But this is all just theoretical. Whoever did this left footprints. Let me do some digging. As soon as we know who's behind this, you can contact your friend."

It wasn't much of a concession, but the idea of being able to call Jack filled her with hope.

Δ Δ Δ

Sara awoke to find Fulbright, sitting in a chair opposite the sofa, quietly watching her. She was accustomed to waking up in strange places, and this was no different. Nevertheless, his scrutiny made her self-conscious. She rubbed her face and ran a hand through her spiky hair, trying to make herself a little more presentable, before acknowledging him.

"How long was I out?"

"A few hours," he replied, with a subdued smile. "I've got some good news and some bad news. And some more bad news."

"Bad news first."

"Actually, let me start with the good news. I know who was behind the attack on the hospital."

She sat up a little straighter. "Do tell."

"An outfit called Manifold Genetics."

"Manifold?" Sara felt her heart skip a beat.

"I take it you've heard of them."

She nodded, but didn't elaborate. "So what's the bad news?"

"Well, that's part of it. Manifold has been involved in some very nasty stuff. Officially, the company was broken up a couple years ago, but that hasn't slowed them down. It turns out, Nexus—the company Felice Carter worked for—was a subsidiary of Manifold. They sent her and her expedition to the Rift to retrieve something, and she succeeded. And now, whatever it was, they have it.

"I managed to get satellite imagery of the area immediately after the attack at the hospital. We caught a break there. With the increase in terrorist activity and piracy in the Horn of Africa, we've got birds overhead. Their helicopter headed due east to a ship anchored in the Indian Ocean. Intel suggests that it's some kind of floating bioweapons development facility. So, not only do they have whatever it is they were after, but they're probably already working on the next phase of their plan:

turning it into a weapon."

Sara shook her head. "If Manifold is behind this, then it's much worse than you can imagine. You have to let me contact Jack—the friend I told you about. He knows all about Manifold. He's the one who took them down."

Fulbright raised an eyebrow. "I'm afraid there isn't time for that. I've been ordered to lead an insertion team onto the ship in order to secure their research."

"And that would be the 'more bad news'?" Sara asked.

"No." His expression turned into a grimace. "I need you to go with me."

When she didn't comment, he hastened to explain his request. "Believe me, I wish there was another way. But you're the only one who's going to be able to make sense of what we find there."

"I'll do it."

Fulbright's eyebrows drew together. "I'm not sure you understand what I'm saying. This action is going to be extremely prejudicial."

"Spare me the spy double-speak. You're going to kill everyone, right? I get it. These bastards killed my friends. And I'm sure whatever they've got planned will kill a whole lot more people. So, am I bothered by the fact that you're going to be 'extremely prejudicial'? Not really." *I'm more worried about what you and your spy friends might be tempted to do with that research once you've got your hands on it*, she thought, but didn't say aloud.

"I'll do everything I can to ensure your safety. You won't go in until the site is secure, but there's still an element of risk."

"I can take care of myself. When do we leave?"

12.

"Ethiopia?"

There was a brief pause and King could almost envision Deep Blue checking the history of his movements from the record of information transmitted by the GPS tracker in his phone.

It was early morning in Addis Ababa, early afternoon in New Hampshire where the new Chess Team headquarters was situated. After checking out the supplies and rented vehicles—two newer model Range Rovers—that Moses had acquired the previous evening, and meeting the four young Ethiopian men he had hired as assistants—King had made a mental note to avoid using the term 'bearers'—he had decided it was time to check in with the home office.

"Well, you have been busy. Two different incidents, and you were right in the middle of both. Care to fill me in?"

"Manifold. They're back in business." King quickly brought Deep Blue up to speed, starting with Sara's mysterious text message, and ending with his decision to accompany Felice Carter back to the Great Rift Valley.

"Is this one of the clones?" Deep Blue asked.

"That's a possibility. I suppose it's also possible that he had so many projects going under different umbrellas that these guys don't know their boss is dead. They might operate autonomously and only involve Ridley when they have something worthwhile to report."

"What do you think they're after this time?" Deep Blue asked.

"I'm still trying to figure that out. I think this started as a fishing expedition, without a clear goal. They just happened to find something important enough to kill for. But that's not why I called."

"Sara."

King took a deep breath. "I need you to find her for me."

There was another period of silence before Chess Team's runner spoke again. "The Ethiopian government is trying to keep this under wraps, but it looks like six bodies were recovered from the hospital."

Six? There had been five CDC scientists in the lab. His heart fell.

"Five were recovered from the first floor, and another—a male—was pulled from a site of a fire on the fourth floor. No identification on any of them yet."

Male? Then he remembered the Gen-Y shooter he had killed in Felice's room; the sixth corpse. "Sara isn't one of them. She was at the hospital when all this went down, but I didn't find her. As far as I know, she's still alive."

"She hasn't checked in with the CDC. Could she have been captured by the Gen-Y team?"

"I don't know." It was a plausible theory, but it just didn't feel right. "I can't imagine what her value to them would be."

"I'm sorry, King."

"I can't think about that right now. I've got to focus on Manifold; figure out what they're up to. But keep looking for Sara, and contact me immediately if you find her."

"Absolutely."

King thumbed the 'end' button and dropped the phone in a pocket. It was time to go.

He found Felice, now wearing blue jeans and a t-shirt, pacing the floor of Moses' residence, like a caged animal. She looked up when he entered, an eager, almost hungry expression on her face. "Now?"

"In a minute. First, I need to know about where we're going. And what you were looking for there."

"That's proprietary information. I'm not at liberty to share it with you."

"In case you weren't paying attention, you got a termination notice yesterday. I don't think you have to worry about a law suit from your former employer. But you're not getting back to that cave without my help, and we don't go anywhere until you start talking."

She returned a pensive frown, not so much bothered by his line of questioning as she was the fact that it was yet another delay. "What do you want to know?"

"Yesterday, you said that you learned of this site from…what was the word you used? 'Esoteric sources'? What did you mean by that?"

"Just that. Instead of relying solely on the verifiable historical record, sometimes we pay attention to local folklore. We don't necessarily take it at face value, but sometimes a pattern emerges, sort of like clues to a treasure map." She resumed pacing the room. "Have you ever heard of the legendary lost graveyard of the elephants?"

"Sounds like something from a Tarzan movie," King remarked.

Felice stopped for a moment, and faced him, her face completely serious. "There's a reason for that. The elephant graveyard is one of those tall tales that has been circulating Africa for centuries, just like King Solomon's Mines or the Kingdom of Prester John. Stories like that tend to take on a life of their own after a while.

"According to the myth, there's a place where all the elephants go when they know they're about to die. They're drawn there, like it's something in their collective subconscious. A lot of dead elephants in one place means a fortune in ivory, just lying there waiting for someone to collect."

"But elephants don't really do that," King said. "I mean, we'd know if they did."

She nodded. "Scientific advancements, both in the field of zoology and remote sensing, have verified that elephants don't behave that way. But when you consider that today's elephant population has been nearly wiped out by poachers and big game hunters, who's to say that something like that wasn't the case a few hundred years ago.

"Most of the stories about the elephant graveyard were easily enough disproven, but one lead was promising because of where it led us: the Great Rift Valley. We know that people have been living in the Rift for hundreds of thousands of years. It made sense that, if there were any truth to the story, then it would have originated there."

"And why was Nexus interested in elephant bones?"

"As I said, the graveyard would be evidence of collective behavior that isn't evident in modern elephants. Our goal was to compare DNA from elephants in the graveyard with that of modern elephants, and hopefully isolate the genetic markers associated with that behavior. If we could identify the section of the elephant genome associated with intelligence, it would go a long way toward understanding the evolution of human consciousness."

King pondered her answer. He didn't get the impression that she was being intentionally deceptive, but her explanation didn't square with his knowledge of Manifold's agenda, nor did it explain why they were willing to kill in order to get control of whatever had been discovered. Finally, he asked: "What about the ape skull that you brought back?"

She gave a helpless shrug, her expression indicating that she was even more bothered by that incongruity than he.

"You've got to remember something," he persisted. "Why

else would you be so insistent on returning?"

"That's just it. I have to go back there to find what I lost."

King considered her answer but he kept coming back to something else she had said. *Drawn there...something in their collective subconscious.*

Is that what's happening to her?

And if what she had found in the cave had awakened some kind of link to a collective subconscious—one that could affect human behavior—what did Manifold have planned for it?

He knew he wasn't going to get those answers from her, and he sensed he was nearing the point where her singular desire to return to the cave would make her less cooperative, more demanding. It was time to get moving.

King drove the lead vehicle, with Felice and Moses as passengers. Felice had not spoken more than a few words since their earlier discussion, and as they drove she simply stared out the window, as if hoping to catch a glimpse of their destination, despite the fact that it lay hundreds of miles to the north. Moses responded to King's questions, but likewise showed little interest in conversation, leaving King alone with his thoughts, which given the uncertainty surrounding Sara's fate, was not a good thing.

As he drove, King's realized that he was scanning the road ahead for signs of an ambush or improvised explosive device placement, habits that had become second nature when he had driven in Afghanistan and Iraq. Ethiopia was no war zone, though there were reports of bandits in remote regions, and intel suggesting a burgeoning *Al Qaida* presence. After the events of the previous day, maybe a little paranoia was a good thing.

While Moses had been out gathering the supplies for the expedition, King had done some shopping as well. He had contacted a more-or-less trustworthy black-market arms dealer, and purchased a used but serviceable Dragunov SVD, equipped with a detachable PSO-1 scope. It wasn't his first choice, but

Russian weapons were more readily available. The sniper rifle's accessories package included a bayonet, which he decided would make a decent substitute for his beloved KA-BAR knife. The dealer had delivered the rifle, along with 500 rounds of 7.62 mm and several boxes of 9 mm rounds for the MP-5. King felt a little better prepared than he had upon arriving in Addis Ababa, but knew that surviving possible future encounters would depend more on good luck and good judgment than on firepower alone. And he already felt like he'd used up a year's worth of good luck.

The day passed uneventfully. They kept to the main highway, traveling north as far as the city of Komolcha, where they ate and refueled, and then traveled east to Semera, the new regional capital of the Afar district. Although there were several hours of daylight remaining, they found lodging and spent the night there. Beyond Semera, there would be little in the way of creature comforts.

Felice seemed to grow more anxious, and more solitary, with each mile traveled. King left her alone. He doubted there was anything more she could tell him, and if there were, it would have to wait until she was ready, until she satisfied the compulsion that was drawing her back to the mysterious cave in the Rift Valley. Moses similarly kept to himself, conversing with the other hired men only to the extent that his duties as translator and de facto expedition manager required him to do so. Like Felice, he also seemed to be in the grip of an external force, not a subconscious homing instinct, but something less specific—the gravity of personal destiny.

King had managed to get the young man to volunteer a little about himself. Moses was a college graduate, but mired in the same economic torpor that kept so many in Africa from rising above the circumstances of their birth. Perhaps, King surmised, he saw the success of this expedition, coming as it did on the heels of the failure of the first, as a way to break that cycle.

That evening, King checked in with Deep Blue, but the conversation was brief; there was nothing to report. No news on Manifold's activities, and no word from Sara. As troubling as the uncertainty was, no news was good news.

They set out the next morning before sunrise, journeying a short distance east to the village of Serdo, then left the highway, heading north on a dirt track that bisected an otherwise empty landscape. It was like driving across the surface of an alien planet.

The Great Rift Valley was an area of intense volcanic and seismic activity. Stretching from Kenya to the Horn of Africa, a distance of thousands of miles, it was the only place on the planet where the earth's tectonic plates moved apart on dry land; all other spreading rifts were submerged deep beneath the oceans. Indeed, the northernmost reaches of the spreading zone that had created the Rift had formed the Red Sea, and in time the valley itself would open up into the Gulf of Aden and be inundated, creating an inland sea. The separation of the plates was almost imperceptibly slow, only a few inches every year— with a few infrequent but extremely dynamic exceptions, such as the 2005 eruption of the Dabbahu volcano, which opened a 37 mile long fissure— but the inevitable process had been going on for millions of years, creating a vast field of featureless lava. Yet, it was not the geological activity which had made this part of the Rift unique, but rather a more recent event, relatively speaking. It was here that fossils of the earliest hominids had been found, the ancestors of modern humans. If prevailing theories were correct, human evolution had turned an important corner here.

King didn't know how the mythic elephant graveyard figured into the tapestry of natural history, but he knew it was no coincidence that Felice Carter had brought back an ape skull.

They drove for hours, road conditions halving the speed they had been able to maintain on the highway, and then early in the afternoon, turned off the road and struck out cross country, their pace further reduced. The distance, according to Moses, was less than a hundred kilometers, but without roads, it would be nearly dusk before they reached their destination.

They saw no one at all; nothing lived or grew in the austere landscape. Nevertheless, King was now fully alert, constantly vigilant for signs of a hostile presence. It seemed likely that Manifold had gotten what it needed from the raid on the hospital, but there was every reason to believe that they might also want to control—or more likely destroy—the source of the genetic material Felice had brought back. He could only hope that, if such were the case, they had already come and gone.

Despite his earlier assurance, as they set out across the roadless landscape, Moses seemed less certain of his ability to find their destination. He claimed to have recognized the spot where the expedition had left the dirt road, and knew the approximate mileage from there to the sight, but in such a vast environment, even a single compass degree of variation might put them miles away from their destination. Without exact coordinates—information Felice had not trusted to memory— even a GPS device would have been useless. But as they traversed the lava field, Felice became more animated, directing him to make course corrections, and King realized that, consciously or not, she was acting as a living GPS, following a powerful and unerring homing instinct.

"How much farther?" he asked, as the vehicle's trip meter hit 95 kilometers.

Felice, who was now barely able to contain her impatience, squinted through the windshield into the darkening eastern sky, and then pointed. "That ridge. The cave is there."

They were close, and soon they would be visible to any watching eyes that might be at the site, especially if the falling dusk required them to use headlights. King drove on a few minutes longer until he spied an elevated area. He pulled to a stop and climbed to the highest point.

The plain that butted up against the ridge was as dark and

featureless as everything else. Using the scope for the Dragunov, he did a visual sweep and managed to pick out the only man-made objects on the landscape, the camp from the original expedition. Although twilight shadows clung to the site like a shroud, he saw no indication of activity—no light, no movement. For some reason, King wasn't as relieved by that as he expected to be.

A few minutes later, the beams of the expedition's headlights illuminated the tattered and burned remnants of the camp. Though only a few days had passed since the events Moses had recounted, the compound looked like the set of a post-apocalyptic movie. Shreds of fabric had snagged on the coils of concertina wire that ringed the compound, and flapped in the breeze like Himalayan prayer flags. Only one of the tents was still standing, looking forlorn amid the wreckage. Two twisted and scorched masses of metal marked the end of what had probably been trucks or SUVs. Everything else was ruined beyond recognition.

Felice seemed uninterested in searching the wreckage. "We need to go to the cave," she insisted. "There's nothing in the camp that will be of any use to us."

Judging by the state of the compound, King was inclined to agree. It seemed very unlikely that any survivors would be found amid the ruins. But where were the bodies?

King shifted his vehicle into drive again, and steered around the wrecked camp, getting closer to the base of the hill. The cave opening was visible, a mere pockmark in the cliff face, and he pulled to a stop a stone's throw away, but not before Felice threw open her door and jumped out.

"Wait!" King shouted after her. "At least let me break out some flashlights." He turned to Moses. "Why don't you have the men set up camp here. I guess Felice and I are going to do a little spelunking."

Moses seemed inexplicably perturbed, but nodded and jumped out to relay the message to the men in the second vehicle. King took an LED MagLite from his duffel bag, along with the MP5, and hurried to join Felice at the mouth of the cave.

As soon as he stepped through the opening, he knew something was wrong. A vile odor permeated the air; a smell of animal excrement mixed with decaying flesh. The flashlight beam revealed dark streaks on the smooth floor of the passage, as if something wet and greasy had been dragged along its length.

"Was it like this before?" King asked.

"I don't remember." Felice's tone was distant and mechanical, as if she had no idea what he was talking about. She quickened her step and it was all King could do to keep up with her.

A short passage led down to an enormous cavern, the depth and breadth of which was beyond the capacity of King's flashlight to illuminate. What he did see in the cone of blue-white light was nevertheless awe-inspiring.

When he had first heard the term "elephant graveyard" he had imagined a place where a few dozen, or maybe even a few hundred skeletons would be jumbled together. But this cavern beggared belief. Directly before him was a veritable sea of gigantic bones and enormous, curving ivory tusks, some at least ten feet in length. The skeletons were packed tightly together, as might occur if individual bodies were stacked one atop another prior to decomposition, and stretched in either direction as far as the eye could see. Without knowing how far back the mass of bones went, it was impossible to estimate the number of skeletons, but it was surely in the thousands, perhaps even tens of thousands.

King understood now why the very idea of an elephant graveyard had galvanized adventurers of the Romantic era to risk everything to find such a treasure. "Incredible. There must be thousands of tons of ivory in here. How much would that be worth anyway?"

Felice ignored his question and instead skirted the cramped area at the perimeter of the bones, disappearing into the shadows. King ran to catch her, casting his light down a path that had been cleared in the bones, and found her all but running to a strange structure—something like a shrine, built entirely of elephant tusks—erected in an open area, deep in the heart of the skeleton maze.

She stopped there, and a few seconds later, he reached her side. "Damn it!" he raged. "You can't run—"

The words died in his throat as something stirred in the shadows. He stabbed the MagLite's beam in the direction of the movement.

To call what he beheld a man was perhaps too generous. The form shambling toward him was indeed human, but only in the strict biological sense. He was naked, except for a few torn remnants of clothes that clung to his body; it looked as if he had tried to simply tear them away, without comprehending the subtleties of buttons and zippers. His matted hair was caked with dirt and his skin was streaked with filth, some of it likely his own excrement. His face was a mask of dried blood, but despite his feral look, his eyes were lifeless, staring unfocused past King to....

To Felice.

He glimpsed movement his left, and swung the light that direction. Another figure was shuffling from the outer perimeter. Then another, and another...seven in all, at least two of them female, but all uniformly bestial in appearance.

And advancing.

Then his light found something else. More remains, but not elephants and not thousands of years old. Piled up behind the shrine was a mass of bodies, bloated and rotting, but not merely left to decompose. Bones were visible where the flesh of the arms and legs had been torn away...gnawed away.

He brought the MP5 up, but knew intuitively that a mere threat would accomplish nothing.

He turned to Felice. "We need to get out of here, now!"

But even as he said it, he realized that her eyes were also drifting, unfocused. And then, even as he was reaching out to grab her arm, she collapsed, like a sacrificial offering laid before the shrine of tusks.

13.

The Indian Ocean, 200 miles southeast of Mogadishu, Somalia

It's like the Brugada incident all over again, Sara thought.

Two years ago, in order to find a cure for a lethal retrovirus that threatened the very survival of the human race, she had left the familiar environs of the research lab, joined a team of lethal Spec Ops warriors, and HALO jumped out of a stealth aircraft into the middle of a free-fire zone.

This felt a lot like that.

Except without Jack.

She and Fulbright had boarded a transport plane in the early hours of the morning following their escape from the hospital, and traveled to Mogadishu, where she was introduced to a team of commandos ostensibly running pirate interdiction operations.

Somalia was a shock to her system. It was everything she had expected Addis Ababa to be; dirty, primitive, a constant assault on her senses. Even sequestered as she was at a highly fortified military style base, surrounded by massive Hesco barriers that looked like the building blocks of an ancient pyramid, the sounds and smells hammered at her. Only her unyielding sense of purpose, in this case, focusing on getting ready to accompany Fulbright in the raid on the floating Manifold lab, allowed her to shut out some of the tumult.

Now, thirty-six hours after arriving in Mogadishu, she was being whisked under the tepid waters of the Indian Ocean. Like the rest of the team, she clung to the exterior of a commercial variant of the Mark VIII Mod 1 Swimmer Delivery Vehicle. The SDV looked like an enormous black torpedo, and had originally been designed to covertly ferry an entire US Navy SEAL dive team and all their gear, to water-borne objectives.

Sara didn't think Fulbright's team were Navy SEALs. She hadn't asked, but her impression was that they were private security contractors, working for the CIA. That probably meant that there were at least a few former SEALs on the team, doing the same job, but presumably for better pay. She had mixed feelings about that. It seemed to be the way things were done in the modern age, but as a civil servant herself, and a close friend of many military personnel, she was uncomfortable with the idea of a paramilitary force that was ultimately motivated only by greed.

She had put these concerns aside in order to focus on the intensive training that would prepare her to accompany the assault team. A certified SCUBA diver, she felt comfortable underwater, but much of the equipment was unfamiliar to her. The team employed Drager LAR-V rebreathers, which utilized carbon scrubbers and a small bottle of pure oxygen to recycle a diver's air in a closed-circuit. The device, worn on the chest, was about the size of a large lunch box, considerably lighter and less bulky than traditional SCUBA tanks. Sara spent nearly two hours getting used to the rebreather, while being towed around by the SDV. There hadn't been time for more than that. The SDV and its future passengers had been loaded aboard a heavily armed support ship, and the mission had gotten underway.

From that point forward, Sara had simply allowed herself

to be carried along, quite literally as was now the case, by forces beyond her control. Her expertise counted for nothing; she was just another piece of equipment the team had to lug around. The passage from the support ship to the target vessel seemed to take hours. In total darkness, enveloped in the soup-warm waters of the Indian Ocean, it was all she could do simply to stay awake.

She knew they had arrived at their destination when the DSV's humming screws stopped turning and the submersible coasted to a stop, but even then, there was nothing to do except wait for Fulbright to give the signal to surface.

Despite her earlier bravado, she was dismayed by the knowledge that, perhaps less than a hundred feet away, people were being killed. It was easy to be sanguine about the death of terrorists and criminals when it took place thousands of miles away; less so, she had discovered from personal experience, when it was happening right in front of you. She had to keep reminding herself that these were the people who had brutally executed her friends, and that given the chance, they would have done the same to her.

The assault team went in from two locations on opposite sides of the vessel. Their movements were guided by a remote surveillance aerial vehicle—a drone—that identified targets and relayed the information in real time to the shooters. With suppressed weapons and night-vision goggles, Fulbright's team visited swift and silent death on the Manifold security team. Less than ten minutes later, Sara felt a tapping on her arm, and knew that the bloody part of the job was finished.

She surfaced to find herself facing a wall of steel. The research ship, which had looked so small and insignificant in satellite imagery, appeared massive up close. Fulbright bobbed next to her, a red-lensed flashlight casting an eerie glow on the dark water and revealing an aluminum scaling ladder hanging from the side of the vessel. Following his lead, Sara scrambled up the ladder, clinging tightly to the rungs, lest her neoprene clad feet lose purchase on the slippery metal. Fulbright was waiting for her at the top, and offered a steadying hand as she clambered over the side rail.

"We've secured the ship," he told her as she stripped off her gear and unzipped her thin wetsuit to allow some of the heat to dissipate. "No friendly casualties. The lab is just below."

Sara hefted the water-tight bag that was her only piece of mission essential equipment. "Lead on."

Guided by radioed instructions from the leader of the commando team, they descended a metal staircase and traversed a short companionway to what looked to Sara like a repurposed cargo hold. But as Sara entered, all sense of being on a marine vessel disappeared. The familiar equipment and computer workstations, illuminated by banks of fluorescent lights, would have looked right at home at the CDC headquarters in Atlanta.

The assault team had found two men working in the lab, and per Sara's request, had managed to take them alive. This was not a matter of mercy or squeamishness on her part; the computers would almost certainly be locked-out, and compelling the prisoners to give them access was critical to the success of the mission. The two scientists, both bearded men about Sara's age, wearing jeans and t-shirts, were presently kneeling with their hands atop their heads, under the watchful eye of the commandos.

Fulbright advanced and introduced himself. "Gentleman, let me get right to the point. You've been doing some very bad things. Developing weapons of mass destruction—"

One of the men started to protest, but Fulbright shushed him as a mother might a wayward child, and kept talking without missing a beat. "It's downright criminal. No, it's worse than that; it's terrorism. And my friends and I have a standing policy when it comes to terrorists: immediate execution.

"You are still alive for one reason, and one reason only. I am going to give you a chance to repent."

Sara had little interest in Fulbright's interrogation methods, and instead began searching the lab to locate the physical products of the ongoing research. Near the center of the compartment, in a sealed Lexan containment chamber, she found the ape skull that had been taken from Felice Carter.

"Now I'm not going to go all Jack Bauer on your ass," Fulbright was saying. "This is simple really. We already have what we want. We'll be taking your computers and all your research back with us, and our techies will be able to hack your passwords and break through your firewalls…whatever it is that they do…and then we'll know everything you know. But see, that takes time, and I'm kind of in a hurry. So here's what I'm offering.

"You're smart guys, right? Educated? You've got special skills that could be very useful. It's not your fault that you wound up working for the wrong side. But that's all over now. You're done working for Manifold. Period. But I'd like to help you find a new job.

"The thing is, I've only got one position available, so think of this as a job interv—"

"I'll do it!" one of the men shouted suddenly. "Please don't kill me."

A murderous look flashed in the eyes of the second scientist. "Dave, you son of a bitch."

Fulbright shushed again. "Dave, is it? You've made the right decision. Welcome to your probationary period. Now, if you'd be so kind, step over here and log on."

Sara tore herself away from the skull and moved over to the workstation where Dave was tapping in his password. She leaned over his shoulder. "Bring up all the files related to your current research."

Dave complied, and as he did, Sara took a portable flash-drive from her bag and plugged it into the USB port. There wasn't time to be choosy about which files to copy, and she knew that workstation probably wouldn't have the really important stuff, like the genome of whatever virus Manifold was monkeying with. Genetic mapping typically required a super-computer with memory measured in terabytes. Sara was primarily interested in the synthesis of their research. She pushed Dave out of the way and started dragging and dropping files into the flash-drive directory.

"That looks interesting," she said, clicking on a file icon that read "Summary Report (draft)."

A text document opened, and despite the fact that it was both a summary and a work in progress, Sara saw that it was more than eighty pages long. She skimmed through it, ignoring the more technical aspects, and tried to get a general overview of what the project was really all about. Words began to leap out at her: retrovirus; evolution; consciousness.

"My God," she whispered. "I know what they're trying to do."

"Well done, Dave," Fulbright said. "Looks like you're hired."

"Son of bitch!"

The scream from Dave's co-worker startled Sara, but not as much as what happened next. The man sprang to his feet and hurled himself across the room. Before he'd taken a single step, a storm of silent lead ripped into him and his chest erupted in a spray of crimson.

The man must have known he would die. Perhaps he had interpreted Fulbright's comment as a tacit pronouncement of his own doom and decided he had nothing left to live for. Whatever the reason, when he decided to make his move, he tapped into his deepest reserves of determination, and when the bullets tore through his vital organs, he kept going. There was only one thing he wanted to accomplish.

Sara saw where he was headed, and in a flash of insight, understood what was about to happen. She had passed the conspicuous looking red button on the way in and recognized it as part of the lab's emergency fail-safe containment system. The CDC employed a similar mechanism, which could be triggered by any number of remote sensor devices, or by a manual device just like that big red button. Evidently, even bioweapons designers were concerned about the accidental release of a deadly pathogen.

Before she could so much as squeak in protest, the man's essentially lifeless body slammed into the button, and the fail-safe was activated. She knew that it would do a lot more than simply sound an alarm.

14.

The Great Rift Valley

Dominance.

    It was the way of the world.

    The Old Mother understood this. There could not be two dominant males in a clan. There could not be two clans in a territory. And though the world itself seemed as vast as the night sky, its limits beyond her ability to grasp, she knew that it was not large enough to sustain two dominant minds.

    For more turnings of the seasons than she could imagine, the great beasts had trod the earth. Their size and strength ensured that the dominance of their common mind would not be shaken. Why they, above all other creatures, had received this gift of wisdom did not concern them any more than the fact that some who shared their blood did not share their thoughts. These latter ones were no threat to the dominance of the great beasts; they were permitted to roam the earth, gathering in herds of their own according to the dictates of their instincts rather than at the guidance of the common mind. But the children of the Old Mother...that was another matter entirely.

The herd could have crushed the Old Mother's clan beneath their feet, torn them asunder with their powerful trunks, impaled them on their mighty tusks. But dominance was not about physical might or even strength of numbers.

No battle would be fought for supremacy, or rather if such a conflict were necessary, it had taken place long before. The herd of great beasts had not assembled in order to contest that outcome, but rather to submit to dominant mind, to the Old Mother.

Lead us, Old Mother.

And she understood.

The time of the great beasts was at an end, as was her own. She had dreamed of a place of death, and now it was time to journey there.

The oldest matriarch gently embraced the Old Mother with its trunk and lifted her onto its back. Then, guided by a single common purpose, the herd began to move again.

They journeyed toward the place where the sun rises, and soon found a land where the rocks burned and the earth bled steam and fire. It was a place where nothing would grow; it was a place of death. With no food or water, many of the herd simply dropped dead in their tracks, but their flesh and blood was offered to the Old Mother for sustenance, and she endured.

On the fourth day, they found the cave.

There was no hesitation. The beasts filed in under the watchful eye of the Old Mother astride the eldest matriarch, and as the sun sank over the distant horizon, only a few of the strongest bulls remained outside, watching reverently as the Old Mother herself at last went in. As soon as she had, they began to use their tusks and trunks to collapse the entrance, sealing their brethren in place of death.

In the darkness, the Old Mother could not see the fate of the herd, but she felt their breath and tasted the air as it grew hot and stale. Sensing that her time had at last come, she lay down and embraced the final sleep....

△ △ △

"Look at this."

"What is that doing here?"

"Primate. An ape of some kind. There's still a lot of preserved tissue. Maybe even some brain matter. I'll bet we can get a viable sample from this."

The Old Mother awakened.

△ △ △

Felice awoke screaming as the memories flooded into her. She saw Sigler, his gun raised, his finger poised on the trigger. Then she saw the others—her friends and co-workers—advancing from the perimeter of the clearing, moving toward her.

She understood everything.

And screamed again.

15.

Manifold laboratory ship, Indian Ocean

A steel door slammed down like a guillotine blade, blocking the only exit from the laboratory. In the same instant, a magnesium charge inside the containment vessel holding the ape skull flared to life. It flamed hot and fast, incinerating the skull and consuming all the available oxygen in the container, and then just as quickly, burned itself out. Then, the strident wailing of a claxon suddenly filled the room.

"What the hell was that?" Fulbright demanded, spinning Dave around to face him.

"It's the fail-safe," Sara supplied before the compliant Manifold researcher could answer. "It's supposed to keep the rest of the ship safe in the event of an accident in the lab."

"Not quite," Dave cut in, his voice quavering. "It does lock down the lab, but it also starts a self-destruct sequence."

"Self destruct?" Fulbright said. "The lab is going to be destroyed?"

Dave shook his head. "Not just the lab; it's already contained. We're not getting out of here. The alarm is to give everyone outside time to abandon ship before…"

"Shit. How long?"

"Five minutes."

Fulbright checked his wristwatch and clicked on a button, before turning to the commandos. "Get that door open."

"It's three inches of solid steel," Dave protested half-heartedly. "We're finished."

"Three inches. Good to know."

The men from the assault team appeared unfazed by the news of the death sentence. They deftly produced blocks of plastic explosives, along with what appeared to be water bladders for hydration packs, and began taping these to the security gate to form a three-foot square. The process took only a few seconds, during which time Fulbright overturned a stainless steel lab table and pulled Sara behind it. Realizing what he intended, she hastily unplugged the flash-drive and stuffed it in the water-tight bag. The commandos joined them, and as soon as they were all down, one of them shouted: "Fire in the hole."

The concussion reverberated through the closed room, hammering into Sara's gut like a punch from a prizefighter, and the smell of high explosives residue made her gums hurt. That she recognized was a manifestation of her SDD.

Fulbright checked his watch before standing up to survey the effects of the breaching charges. "We've got three minutes people. Move."

The shaped explosive charges had done the trick, blasting an opening in the steel gate, large enough for one person at a time to crawl through. Without asking, Fulbright propelled Sara forward, and she hastily pulled herself through the still smoldering hole.

Once outside, Fulbright wasted no time. He grabbed Sara's elbow and started running back the way they had come, shouting instructions to the rest of the team into his radio. Sara headed for the ladder where she'd left her rebreather, but Fulbright forestalled her.

"No time for that."

She gaped, uncomprehending, as he raced past their equipment, and moved instead to row of large cylindrical containers mounted along the ship's superstructure. Moving with what looked like practiced efficiency, Fulbright worked a lever handle, and the cylinder burst from its stays and flew out over the side.

"Jump!"

Sara hesitated, still trying to grasp what was happening. Fulbright didn't bother with an explanation, but simply grabbed her shoulders and propelled her over the rail. She clutched instinctively for a handhold, but it was too late. Arms flailing, she dropped thirty feet into the warm ocean.

The impact stunned her, knocking the wind from her lungs, but somehow Fulbright was there, hugging her body to his and kicking furiously back to the surface. Everything that followed was a blur.

A resounding thump jolted her back to awareness, and she realized that she was no longer in the water. She jumped, like someone waking from a dream of falling, and saw that she was in some kind of rubber boat. Fulbright was sitting next to her, panting like he'd just finished a marathon. A greenish glow surrounded them, courtesy of a Cyalume chemical light stick.

"Are you alright?" he asked.

Sara tried to speak, but the words wouldn't take shape, so she simply nodded.

Fulbright took a few more breaths. "Okay, that was close." He gazed at her thoughtfully. "Did you get anything useful?"

Sara instinctively felt for the waterproof bag with the flash-drive. It was still there, slung over her shoulder. But the mere fact of its presence was no cause for rejoicing. She turned to Fulbright. "I managed to download their research reports," she said, at length. "I know what they were trying to do, but without a sample of the virus they were working with, the information isn't much good."

A noise like the rushing of river rapids made further comment impossible. She craned her head around in time to see the bow of the research vessel, its lower hull shot full of holes from the detonation of Manifold's self-destruct device—the source of the thump she had heard a moment before—abruptly tilt upward and then slide beneath the surface. The otherwise placid sea roiled with whirlpools of cavitation, but in a matter of seconds, all trace of the research vessel was gone. Three other lifeboats bobbed in the water nearby, but in the darkness it was impossible to tell how many of the commandos had made it off.

Sara sagged back against the vulcanized rubber gunwale, overcome by fatigue as the adrenaline drained from her bloodstream. Several minutes passed before it occurred to her to feel a sense of relief at having survived the ordeal.

Finally, she sat up and elaborated. "That ape skull was from an Australopithecine female."

"Australia?"

Sara shook her head. "Australopithecus was one of the primate species that eventually evolved into Homo sapiens. It's one of the fabled 'missing links' between apes and humans. The skull contained a retrovirus, which Manifold believed was responsible for the mutation that gave rise to human consciousness."

"I don't understand. A virus is responsible for turning apes into humans?"

"It's more complicated than that, but essentially, yes. Viruses are just strands of genetic material that use our cells to replicate themselves. Certain viruses—retroviruses—actually alter the DNA of the cells that they invade. That's the basis for gene therapy. It's theoretically possible to introduce a virus that would rewrite a person's entire genome. As new cells are created by mitosis, they would all carry the new DNA, and over time, every cell in a person's body would be produced with the new code. That's the theory, but in practice, it's almost impossible. There are just too many cells in the body, and the natural response of the immune system would either fight the virus or kill the host.

"Manifold postulated that such a virus was responsible for adding the section of the genetic code that triggered self-awareness. From what I could gather, their working hypothesis was that an early hominid was exposed to the virus in utero, when the cells were still undifferentiated. That allowed for the mutation to completely alter the embryo's DNA without triggering an immune response. When the child was born, the mutation would have enabled it to make to quantum leap to a rudimentary form of human consciousness, which it in turn passed on to its offspring. The section of the genetic code supplied by that retrovirus is in every human alive today. It seems that skull belonged to our common great-many times over-grandmother."

Fulbright's forehead creased with a frown. "If the virus is what evolved us into humans, how would it be a danger today? How could they use it as a weapon?"

Sara bit her lip thoughtfully. "I think they were trying to figure out a way to switch off that gene. Maybe by a secondary exposure to the virus."

"Switch it off? That would…what? Turn us all into mindless apes?"

She nodded grimly. "I think that was the general idea."

Fulbright let out a low whistle. "Can they do it? More importantly, is there a way to develop a vaccine to keep that from happening?"

"They would have had to do the genetic sequencing off-site, using a Cray supercomputer. So even though this lab was destroyed, we have to assume that they have the genome for the virus, and maybe even a viable sample that they can culture. To develop a vaccine, we would also need a sample of the original virus."

"And where are we going to get that?"

"From the source." She tapped the bag with the flash-drive. "We need to go where Felice Carter found that skull. We need to get there now. "

16.

The Elephant Graveyard, Afar District, Ethiopia

King eased his finger off the trigger and glanced at Felice from the corner of his eye. He couldn't tell whether she was telling him not to shoot, or screaming at the zombie-like figures shambling toward them. Regardless of her intent, both happened; he checked his fire and the zombies froze in place. He kept the MP5 trained on the nearest one a few moments longer, but none of them so much as blinked.

It was actually kind of creepy.

"What just happened?" he asked, without turning to look at Felice.

He realized that she was sobbing. "I did this. To them. I made them that way."

His first impulse was to console her with words of denial, but he knew such claims would offer little comfort. She knew what had happened; somehow, she just knew, and if she believed that she was somehow responsible for turning the others into cannibalistic beasts, that was something he could ill-afford to dismiss. "Felice, honey, whatever has happened, we can talk it about it later. Right now, what do you say we just move very slowly back outside?"

She let out another wet sob then sniffed loudly. "No. It's all right. They'll do whatever I tell them."

"O-kay," King answered slowly. "But if it's all the same to you, I think I'd prefer to discuss this somewhere else."

Felice got to her feet, ignoring King's extended helping hand, and walked toward one of the men. She stopped directly in front of him, and then reached out and placed her hand on his cheek. The man didn't react at all. "This is Bill Craig. He was a zoologist. He also liked to write science-fiction stories."

She lowered her hand and moved to another of the motionless figures. "This is Wayne Skiver. He was the lead geneticist. He was also planning to open his own restaurant someday."

King noticed her conspicuous use of the past tense. "Felice. This wasn't your fault. Let's get out of here."

"It was my fault. I found it. I *unleashed* it." She filled the words with such anger that King felt a chill shoot down his back.

"What did you find?"

"A ghost. An evil spirit. The Old Mother. She drove these elephants into the cave four hundred thousand years ago. And when I found her, she destroyed their minds, took control of my friends; Bill, Wayne...all of them." She turned back to him. "I know you won't believe me, but I can feel her in me."

King strode cautiously over to stand in front of her, just as she had done with her co-workers. He took her hand in his. "Felice, I don't know if I believe in ghosts, but I'm sure we can find some way to deal with this. Let me help you."

This time she complied, but the look she gave him was one of resignation, not gratitude. King didn't really care, as long as it got her moving. They moved away from the shrine and down the path through the bones. The seven zombies remained still as statues behind them.

He had hoped that her distress would ease once away from the shrine, but it was not to be. "Did you see the bodies?" she asked as they negotiated the tunnel back to the surface. "They turned into cannibals. My fault. All my fault."

He grabbed her by the shoulders. "Felice. You're a scientist; think about this rationally. Something caused it to happen; a virus or a prion or something. That's what you've got to focus on; that's what Manifold wants to control. And if they can figure out how it works, then they can make other people like that."

She gazed past him, unresponsive. He decided to try a different tack.

"Felice. That's who you are; Felice Carter. Where did you say you're from? Somewhere in Washington state?"

"Kirkland," she murmured.

"That's near Seattle, right? Have you been to the Space Needle."

A laugh escaped her lips, cracking the mask of despair. "That's for tourists."

King smiled. "Well, I'll tell you what. When you're back home in Kirkland, I'll come visit you and you can take me to the Space Needle."

"Elvis," she said, unexpectedly. "Your shirt."

"Yeah? What about it?"

"I'll take you to the Experience Music Project. You might like that."

"It's a date." He grinned. It was working; he'd broken through whatever spell she was under. "Right now, though, we need to figure out what happened to you in there. Can you do that?"

Her face clouded again, but she nodded.

"Something happened when you found that skull, right? You were exposed to something?"

"Maybe. But what I saw...that wasn't from any virus."

"What did you see?"

He listened as she struggled to find words to express what she had seen and experienced—a vision of a proto-human woman and her evolution of consciousness, and how that had led to the mass death of thousands of elephants, more than four hundred millennia previously. "Those memories didn't come from exposure to a pathogen," she concluded. "Don't you see? I was...*possessed*, somehow. And it spread to the others; I was controlling them, just like she controlled those elephants."

"What if there's another explanation?" King was desperate to find that alterative, but he was out of his depth. Sara would have known. "Isn't there such a thing as genetic memory? Animals are born knowing how to do some things, right? Birds follow migration patterns to places they've never been before.

"When you first told me about the elephant graveyard, you mentioned collective behavior. What if this is a manifestation of that?"

Her brows knit together in contemplation, but he could tell that she was finally thinking rationally again. "I suppose it could be something like that."

"Now, tell me what Manifold would want with something like that."

She pondered this for a moment, and then her eyes grew wide. "Control. Turn people into robots, or mindless zombies like..." She gestured back down the passage.

"Good girl. Figuring out what they're after is the first step toward fighting it." He gently turned her so that she was facing the mouth of the cave. "Now, let's get out—"

The words died along with his brief elation as he saw the barrel of an AK-47 aimed at his chest.

17.

The Russian-designed Kalashnikov rifle was the first thing King saw. The weapon attracted his gaze like a magnet, but he forced himself to look up, into the eyes of the man that held it.

It was one of the Ethiopian workers they had hired in Addis Ababa. A second man, also from that group and likewise armed, advanced and quickly relieved King of his MP5, then shoved King toward the exit, barking an order—presumably in Amharic—that required no translation. King raised his hands in a show of compliance, and moved out of the cave, with a wide-eyed Felice right next to him.

The other two Ethiopian hired men were waiting outside with Moses, and while the men were armed, King noted that Moses did not appear to be under guard. "What's going on here, Moses?"

Night had descended over the valley and it was hard to see the young man's expression, when he spoke, there was a hint of regret in his voice. "I have been in the cave. I have seen the treasure of ivory; a treasure that belongs to the people of Ethiopia, to all Africans."

"Ivory?" Felice asked, incredulous. "You're doing this for the ivory?"

"The ivory is a means to an end. But it is also emblematic of the very reason that such action is necessary. Ivory, like gold, diamonds, and oil, is one of Africa's great natural resources that has been plundered for centuries to enrich the coffers of foreign kings, while leaving the indigenous people to wallow in poverty, or worse, be enslaved by those foreigners."

King thought the speech sounded rehearsed, but he did not interrupt.

"This must change," Moses continued. "The wealth of Africa must be used to enrich the people of Africa, starting with the ivory in the cave.

"Did you know that, despite an international ban on the sale of ivory, the wholesale slaughter of elephants continues. The elephants are on the verge of extinction, and yet foreigners continue to buy ivory. My kinsmen, desperate for money, facilitate the slaughter, but it is the foreign ivory brokers who reap the reward. When news of this discovery reaches the world, those foreigners will act swiftly to take control of this place in order to secure their own prosperity—just as the cartel has done with diamonds—and nothing will change. That cannot be allowed to happen."

"So you want to ensure control of the ivory for your own people," King said. "I get that. It's a noble endeavor. But this isn't the way to go about it."

"You misunderstand. We will use this treasure to buy back our freedom, to break the chains of foreign oppression."

King's eyes widened in comprehension. "You're going to use it to finance a revolution."

"These men," Moses gestured to the armed Ethiopians, "are soldiers in the Pan-African Army of Freedom. Yes, they are revolutionaries, but they do not seek merely to topple on corrupt government and replace it with another. They desire, as do I, an end to the control of Africa's wealth and people, by foreign interests. The era of colonial Africa will end. We will see it done."

"Let me guess. They'll make you president for life."

Moses chuckled. "I have no such ambition. Besides, the struggle will be long, but in time, it will be up to the people of Africa to elect a capable leader. Someone untainted by corruption and the influence of foreign corporations."

"Do you really believe you could ever get them all to agree to that? Get all the different tribes and ethnic groups to put aside centuries of conflict?"

Moses' voice suddenly took on a harsh edge. "Who do you really believe is responsible for tribal violence and ethnic cleansing? Foreign powers have continued to set brother against brother, playing on superstitious fears in order to keep their control, and when tragedy occurs, they stand back and say: 'Look, the Africans are savages who cannot rule themselves.' Do not presume to lecture me on the matter of African history."

Felice spoke up. "Moses, I agree with you. I think what's been happening here is terrible. And you're right. The wealth of Africa should be used to help Africans first. But there's more going on here than you realize."

Moses made a cutting gesture with his hand. "Do not think that because you have black skin, you are any different. I know who you are, who you work for. Your company sent you here to find this place; to pillage yet another of our natural resources."

"No," she pleaded. "I mean, maybe that's why we came here in the first place. But there's something dangerous in that cave. Something evil."

"You will not sway me with superstition." He snorted derisively, but King thought there had also been a note of hesitation in the young man's response.

He knows. King realized. *He went in the cave to rescue Felice; he had to have seen what it did to the others.* "It's not superstition. You know what she's talking about. You saw what it did to her. They found something in there; some kind of pathogen."

Moses turned to one of the gunmen and said something in their shared language. Then he addressed King and Felice again. "My friends would like to see what you have discovered. Perhaps you can show us this evil you speak of."

△ △ △

King's hands were bound behind his back. He realized as the knots were cinched tight that he'd probably missed several opportunities to overpower his captors. Moses' betrayal had caught him completely off guard, but rather than berate himself for his failures, he instead determined to be ready when the next chance presented itself. The four gunmen were not professional soldiers—he could tell that much just by watching their behavior—and while that didn't necessarily make them any less dangerous, it would give him an advantage when he made his move. Lacking military discipline and reflexes sharpened by training and combat, they would hesitate, perhaps only for a fraction of a second, and that would be all the time he needed. For the moment, however, he did not resist. He needed them to believe that their control was absolute.

Using the powerful electric lanterns from their supplies, the party moved back into the cave. Moses and the four gunmen exchanged a few words in their common tongue, and King used the opportunity to reassure Felice. "Everything is going to be all right," he told her, his voice barely above a whisper. "If something happens, just get down and cover up."

She looked back at him, her eyes full of fear and not as much hope as he would have liked, and nodded slowly.

In the diffuse light from the lanterns, everything looked different. King was awed by the number of elephant skeletons stacked up in the cavern. All African elephants, male and female alike, grew tusks, so the amount of ivory contained in the chamber was beyond comprehension; probably more than the sum total of all that had been harvested from hunting in recorded history. King didn't know much about the current state of the ivory market; was there even a demand for it anymore?

That might be something to use as leverage against Moses, but King suspected the young idealist was beyond reason. As long as there were guns pointed at him, reasoning with Moses and the others wasn't high on King's list of priorities.

After about half an hour of marveling over the sheer scope of the ivory trove, during which time King and Felice were constantly guarded by two gunmen, the group moved back up the passage to the surface. The Ethiopians had not ventured beyond the outer perimeter, and King got the distinct impression that Moses was purposely avoiding the path that led to the shrine of tusks.

King noticed a change in the demeanor of the four armed revolutionaries. They seemed emboldened by their newfound wealth, louder and more aggressive. King also saw a growing look of dismay on Moses's face.

"Problem with your new friends?"

Moses glared back at him angrily. "They are trying to decide whether to hold you and Felice for ransom, or simply execute you."

"Yeah? What's your vote?"

"This isn't what I wanted. There wasn't supposed to be any violence."

King laughed humorlessly. "You thought maybe you could free Africa from foreign domination by asking politely?"

Moses winced as if the comment had been a physical blow. "That's not what I meant."

"You need to get control of this situation," King pressed. "Senseless violence is no way to launch your dream of a free Africa. It just confirms what everyone already says; that you are savages."

The young Ethiopian's eyes were like daggers. King knew

his harsh words had struck the right nerve, but he also knew that they were probably already past the point where Moses might be able to reason with his confederates.

As if to underscore King's suspicion, one of the men abruptly grabbed Felice's arm and dragged her away like chattel. King's muscles bunched, reflexively struggling against his bonds, but as he started after Felice's abductor, another of the rebels rammed the wooden stock of an AK into his gut. King saw the blow coming and managed to turn his body just enough to avoid serious injury, but the assault doubled him over and put him on his knees.

Moses seemed paralyzed by the sudden violence, but as Felice began struggling in her captor's grip, he overcame his shock and leapt to her rescue. He got a hand on the man's shoulder before the rebel who had clubbed King went after him, thrusting him aside disdainfully. The other two rebels cheered their comrade on, covering both Moses and King with their rifles.

As he tried to get his feet back under him, King saw the look of despair in Moses' eyes; the realization that his carefully laid plans had gone up in a blaze of lust and violence. He had delivered the prize to the freedom fighters, expecting to be embraced as their visionary leader, but now he was simply in their way.

King knew he had only a few seconds in which to act, to do something, anything, to prevent the men from gang raping Felice, and probably killing him as well. Moses, willing though he now appeared to be, probably wasn't going to be much use in a fight. Nevertheless, the young man's ill-conceived attempt at chivalry had diverted the attention of the rebels, if only for a moment, and King wasn't going to let that moment go to waste.

He lowered his head and somersaulted toward the rebel guarding him. The AK cracked loudly as a bullet split the air where he had been an instant before, but before the man could adjust his aim, King, with his back flat against the ground, drove both feet up into the man's gut.

As the man staggered backward, King was moving again, using his bound hands to push off the ground and spring to his feet. But even as he moved, he saw the other rebels' guns tracking him, and knew that he'd lost whatever advantage he'd had.

Then Felice screamed, and he realized that getting shot by the rebels just might be the least of his worries.

18.

King could see, in his mind's eye, the seven zombie-like members of the original research team, rushing from the depths of the cave, responding to the threat to Felice. They were like warrior bees, instantaneously mobilizing to defend the queen.

But before that could happen, the man assaulting Felice abruptly fell back, as if he had received an electrical shock. He then got to his feet, and turned woodenly toward his comrades. Although the latter were poised to shoot King, their eyes were drawn to the would-be rapist. There was no fear in their eyes; instead, they seemed amused, as if they thought their friend was playing a joke. King knew better; in the icy white glow of the electric lantern, he could see that Felice's assailant now wore the same blank expression as the zombies in the cave.

Moses must have noticed it as well, for he scrambled back as if the approaching man was a venomous serpent. The man ignored him and advanced toward his comrades—*former comrades,* King thought—his face and body language betraying nothing of his intent. One of the rebel fighters said something in Amharic, perhaps asking for an explanation for the odd behavior, but none of the three Ethiopians seemed to sense that something had gone very wrong.

The only answer came in the form of an attack. The changed man approached the closest rebel and started raining blows with closed fists.

The rebels stumbled back, gripped by confusion, and for a moment did nothing to intervene. The punches were brutal, filled with primal energy, and the target of the attack was rendered senseless before he could so much as raise a hand in his own defense. The two remaining rebels, still unable to process what was happening, leapt forward to restrain the man, but he wrestled free of their hold and began directing his fury at them.

At last, the two rebels seemed to understand that their friend now meant to kill them, and as one of them also went down under a rain of fists, the remaining man brought his Kalashnikov rifle to bear. He took a couple steps back, and then took aim.

Before he could pull the trigger however, reinforcements arrived. The seven zombies emerged from the cave and descended on the gunman like warrior ants. The rifle discharged with a thunderous crack, but the bullet zipped away into the night sky as the man went down under the combined weight of his assailants. From the midst of the tangle of bodies came the sickening crunch of bones breaking.

All of this happened in a matter of seconds, time in which King sorted through his options like a bad hand in a poker game. Moses had fled the scene, running flat out toward the parked SUVs. He would be no help, but despite his betrayal, King wasn't ready to count the young idealist as an enemy. Felice was probably safe; the zombies had come in response to a threat to her safety. Their sole purpose seemed to be protecting her from harm, but King got the impression that they no longer possessed any ability to discriminate friend from foe.

But in the cave, they had responded to her commands; would that work again? Or would approaching Felice make him the primary target of the zombies' wrath?

As he pondered this, he contorted his body and threaded

his legs through the circle formed by his bound wrists. There was no time to wrestle with the knots, but with his hands now in front of him, he would be able to use them in his own defense. It wouldn't count for much if all seven—make that eight—of the zombies attacked en masse.

He jogged over to where Felice lay. She was sobbing, but did not appear to be in the grip of another episode of catatonia. He knelt beside her. "Felice. It's okay now. You're safe."

She looked up at him, her eyes wild in the grip of an adrenaline fugue, but after a moment she began looking around to verify what he was telling her.

"You're safe now," he repeated. The sound of footsteps scrabbling on the hard lava rock signaled that his actions had not gone unnoticed. "No one is going to hurt you. But you need to call them off."

"Call them…?"

"The zombies." He winced at his use of the term, but didn't know what else to call them. "Tell them to stop. Send them back to the cave."

Comprehension dawned. She glanced over his shoulder at the approaching horde and raised a hand.

The crunch of footsteps stopped immediately and an eerie silence descended over the plain. King looked back cautiously and saw the group arrayed around him, only a few feet away. He breathed a tentative sigh of relief, but when he looked back at Felice, all he saw was horror. Her eyes were riveted on the form of the man who had, only a few moments earlier, been trying to rape her.

"What have I done?" she whispered, hoarsely. "I did that to him. I made him that way."

"You protected yourself."

She shook her head, and then hugged her arms around her torso as if fighting back a wave of nausea. "I thought that it was something that happened to all of us when we found the remains in the cave…that we were all changed by what we had discovered…but that's not…it was me. I did this to them. I destroyed their minds." She looked into King's eyes again. "I can't control this."

"Yes you can." He put every ounce of certainty he could muster into his tone, but deep down he wasn't sure at all. "You didn't change me. You were being hurt and you fought back. That's all. You have to believe that."

He could tell that his words failed to convince her, but it was a start.

"We should get out of here," he said, rising to his feet. "You have some answers now; you know what happened. There's nothing more for you here."

She considered this for a moment, her eyes still fixed on the semi-circle of motionless zombies, then gave a weak nod. As if responding to the gesture, the group abruptly turned and filed back into the cave.

Relieved, King finally turned his attention to the ropes that bound his wrists. The knots were pulled tight, but appeared to be fairly simple. He tugged them loose with his teeth, and in a matter of seconds, was able to wriggle free. He then helped Felice to her feet and together they moved toward the parked vehicles.

Moses was waiting for them, his hands spread in a gesture of contrition. "Please," he said, as if to forestall an act of retribution. "I never meant for that to happen. You were not to be harmed."

King wasn't sure how to respond, but to his surprise, Felice spoke first. "I believe you. And I understand why you felt you had to do this. I wish you had told us what you wanted in the first place. It would have prevented all of this from happening."

Moses was as speechless as King.

"The cave is dangerous," Felice continued. "I know you believe that it represents a source of wealth for the future of Africa, but it's not safe. You must see that."

He nodded dumbly.

She held out a hand to him. "I haven't forgotten that you rescued me once. I remember it all now. Let me return the favor."

Almost tentatively, the young Ethiopian took the proffered hand. King kept his expression neutral, doing his best to hide his reservations. He doubted that they had anything more to worry about from Moses, but a betrayal was nonetheless a betrayal. And there was no telling how far the ripples of that action would spread.

As if to underscore what he was thinking, the unmistakable sound of helicopter turbines—distant but nevertheless growing closer—became audible. King scanned the horizon in all directions and quickly located two sets of green and red aircraft lights approaching from the east.

It was of course highly unlikely that the helicopters belonged to the Pan African Army of Freedom, or any other ragtag rebel group, but that was of little comfort to King. As far as he knew, there was only one other group that knew the location of the cavern: Felice's former employers at Nexus/Manifold.

For the first time since getting free of his bonds, it occurred to King that he had not armed himself. He had no idea what had become of his MP5. The bodies of the three rebel fighters, and the AK-47s they had wielded, lay some fifty meters away. The Dragunov rifle was presumably still in its case in the SUV, but there almost certainly wasn't enough time to break it out and assemble it before the helicopters arrived. Even the attempt might provoke a hostile response; it was a sure bet that they were already under scrutiny from observers in the aircraft.

"Change of plans," King declared. "Back to the cave."

Felice was visibly shocked at the suggestion. "What?"

"No time to explain." He took her hand and began striding purposefully across the open area toward the mouth of the cave.

It was already too late. One of the craft swooped down

between them and their destination, flaring its rotors and buffeting them with a blast of artificial wind. King held up a hand, partly to deflect some of the grit that was blasting into his face, and partly to shade his eyes from the high intensity spotlight that stabbed out from the helicopter, transfixing him and Felice like bugs on a pin. The message was crystal clear: stay put. There didn't seem to be any alternative.

But then, as the turbines were shut down, returning the night once more to silence, King heard a familiar voice reach out from the center of the blazing light. "Jack? Is that really you?"

19.

It was difficult to say who was more surprised at the reunion. Sara rushed forward, and in an uncharacteristic display of emotion, wrapped her arms around King. She felt cold to the touch and her kiss tasted faintly of salt, but he welcomed it nonetheless. Days of uncertainty about her fate had been swept aside, and all the questions about what had happened seemed completely unimportant.

When he at last drew back from her embrace, he got a look at her traveling companions, most of whom had deployed in a defensive perimeter around the two helicopters. They all, Sara included, wore dark fatigues, but aside from Sara, only one man was not openly wielding some kind of weapon. That lone hold-out was a handsome dark-haired man, who seemed to be waiting for Sara to make an introduction.

"So you must be the friend that Sara told me about," he intoned. "Jack, is it? I'm Max Fulbright."

King nodded, and cast an inquisitive glance in Sara's direction. Her expression told him that she had volunteered only the barest minimum of information about him. "That's right. Generally speaking, Sara and I try not to interfere in each other's work, but sometimes there's a bit of overlap."

"This time there's a lot," Sara said. "Manifold Genetics is involved, Jack. And you'll never guess what they've been up to."

"Actually, I might." King beckoned Felice forward. "I don't know if you got a chance to meet her back in Addis, but this is Felice Carter."

Sara did a double-take as she recognized the geneticist. "Last time I saw you…" She left the sentiment hanging as something else dawned in her eyes. "Jack, she could be infected."

King shook his head. "It's much worse than that."

He gave a quick synopsis of everything that had happened from the moment he rescued Felice from the burning hospital room, up to their arrival at the cavern. Felice seemed visibly pained by what he was saying, but the information was too important for him to sugar-coat anything. When he was done, Sara turned to Felice.

"I've been to the Manifold lab where they were trying to exploit what you found, and I've seen their research. They want to isolate the contagion that causes this…" She turned back to King, "zombie state. It's the key to all of this, and she may have it in her."

"I don't think it's that simple," King countered. "There's something else at work here." He glanced at Felice, then took Sara aside and in a low voice, described what had happened when the rebels had tried to assault Felice. "She changed him," he explained. "Just like that. One second he was attacking her, and the next, he was a mindless drone. That wasn't the result of exposure to a contagion."

Although he hadn't been invited into the conversation, Fulbright spoke up. "Are you saying that she's doing it…changing people with some kind of supernatural power?"

King glanced at Sara, curious to see her reaction to that suggestion. "I don't know what the mechanism is, but I know what I saw."

"Then we've got to keep her safe," Fulbright declared. "I'll arrange for transport to a secure facility."

As Fulbright moved to the nearest helicopter, King turned back to Sara. "Who is that guy?"

"I think he's CIA."

"You're not sure?"

She shrugged. "You know how spooks can be. But he arranged the takedown of a Manifold lab. He's trying to get out in front of whatever they've got planned."

"I don't trust him."

Sara playfully punched his shoulder. "Jack, are you jealous?"

He offered a half-hearted grin. "Guilty as charged. But seriously, this is some bad shit. I don't trust anyone right now, least of all the Company."

"I don't know if we have any other options right now. If what you say is true—if she's not in control of this...this ability—then we've got to keep her under wraps."

Sara took a breath then continued. "I don't buy into this idea of psychic power, but there are any number of other ways this might have happened. The research we took from the Manifold lab indicates that the virus they discovered here might have been responsible for the genetic mutation that led to the rise of human consciousness hundreds of thousands of years ago. They thought a second exposure to the virus might switch that gene off, essentially reversing that evolutionary leap. But maybe the trigger is something else. A pheromone that she releases when threatened. Just imagine how that could be used as a weapon. We've got to isolate exactly what that trigger is so we can come up with a way to stop it, and if we're lucky, reverse the process."

"She's not a lab rat, Sara."

Something dark and angry flashed in Sara's eyes. "No. She's patient zero for an outbreak that just might wipe out humanity, and that's exactly how I have to think of her. You of all people should know that sometimes saving the world requires sacrifices. Hope and good vibrations aren't going to save us from this, Jack. Let me do my job."

Before King could respond, Fulbright returned. "It's all arranged. Miss Carter, if you could just come with me."

Felice lurched into motion as if the events of the past few days and recognition of her own role in those events had, at long last, deprived her entirely of volition. She moved, almost like one of the zombies, toward the waiting helicopter. As she stepped past Fulbright, he grasped her biceps with one hand.

Felice let out a cry of surprise and pulled away, clapping a hand to her arm where he had touched her. King caught a glimpse of a hypodermic syringe in the man's hand.

Fulbright stepped back hastily, raising both hands. "Just something to make sure she doesn't change all of us into zombies."

"That's completely unnecessary," Sara accused. "You should have asked me first."

"My apologies, Dr. Fogg, but you're not calling the shots anymore." Fulbright lowered his hands, letting the syringe fall, and then stepped forward to catch Felice as the sedative he had administered went to work.

Moses suddenly jumped forward, breaking his long silence, and tried to wrestle Felice's limp form away, but Fulbright shoved him back with his free hand, and then in the same motion drew a pistol and pointed it at the young Ethiopian. Moses raised his hands in a show of surrender, but the gesture evidently made no impression on Fulbright.

He calmly pulled the trigger, and shot Moses between the eyes.

20.

Sara gasped as the small pistol roared and the young Ethiopian man's head snapped back. Right up to that moment, things had more or less made sense, and even now, her brain tried to wrestle with what she had just witnessed, to figure out how it fit with everything else.

But it just didn't. Fulbright had murdered someone in cold blood, and now his gun was swinging toward Sigler. In the corner of her eye, she saw the other members of Fulbright's assault team shoulder their weapons, likewise taking aim at her boyfriend.

Sigler was already moving. Maybe his stated distrust of Fulbright had given him just enough of an edge to act decisively when the betrayal occurred. Sara saw him zigzagging across the open area, and then the world seemed to explode in a haze of noise and sulfur smoke. She couldn't tell if Sigler had been hit, and before she could find him again, one of the commandos grabbed her by the shoulder and propelled her toward the helicopter. Fulbright was already stuffing the unconscious Felice into one of the rear seats.

He looked at Sara as he buckled Felice's safety harness over her torso. "Sit down and shut up, Dr. Fogg. You've got important work to do, and I hope for your sake that you'll be cooperative. I will get what I want either way; it's just a question of how hard you want to make it for yourself."

Still reeling from the violence and treachery, Sara complied without really even knowing what she was doing.

Fulbright leaned out and addressed the commando. "Did you get him?"

The man shook his head. "Might have wounded him, but he made it to that cave."

"Keep a team here and make sure he's dead."

A pang shot through Sara's heart at the pronouncement. Fulbright reached back tapped the pilot's shoulder, signaling him to start the engines, and then he settled into his own seat and buckled in. She had to understand what she had just witnessed. It was the only way to keep the despair at bay, to keep from thinking about what she had just witnessed, and... *Jack*!

"Who the hell are you?" she demanded, shouting to be heard over the whine of the turbine.

He stared at her, a hint of his roguish smile returning. He reached forward and settled a headset over her ears. The cushioned earphones dramatically reduced the engine noise. Fulbright donned a set as well.

"That's better." His expression was sardonic, but somehow the electronic amplification of the intercom failed to convey it in his tone. "Who am I? I told you my name. There's really not much more to tell."

"You're not CIA, are you?"

He laughed. "I never said I was, though in point of fact, I am a field officer with the Company. But it just so happens that..." He glanced at the ceiling as if searching for the right word. "You might say I'm moonlighting. But I'm not going to talk about that."

There was a lurch as the helicopter lifted off. Sara felt her stomach drop as the pilot tilted the aircraft forward and swooped away, but she fought back the waves of nausea. "You said I should cooperate. That works both ways."

He crossed his arms. "Believe it or not, I haven't told you anything that isn't true. My employer knew what Manifold was trying to do, and wanted to develop a cure or a vaccine; something to permanently remove that threat. As my employer might say, you have the highest probability of finding that cure."

"Your employer, would that be the Russians? The Chinese? No, I'm sure you're a patriot; you'd never do that. A rival genetics firm, then? I won't help you turn this thing into a bioweapon, no matter how much you torture me."

Fulbright laughed. "I don't think my employer is interested in developing bioweapons. There's no profit in it."

"So it is just about money?"

"It's always just about money." He regarded her across the dimly lit interior, as if weighing how much more to reveal. "Let me tell you how the world really works.

"Nations, armies, governments…they don't mean anything anymore. They don't have any power anymore. Everything is controlled by corporations. And unlike governments and armies, corporations don't make decisions based on whims or idealistic beliefs or petty revenge. They are motivated by just one thing; the need to keep growing. They are, in a very real sense, a higher life form. The individual shareholders might be governed by those petty human concerns, but that all gets lost in the collective decision making process. They are like brain cells, and in the end, no matter what the individuals may think or believe, the corporation is driven by the singular desire to make a profit. It's a paragon of efficiency.

"I called it a life form; I wasn't joking about that. You see, something happened a couple decades ago. No one really knows all the details, but the working theory is that the quest for greater efficiency led to the creation of a vast computer network called Brainstorm."

"You expect me to believe that a computer is running the world?" Sara scoffed. "That's pure science fiction."

"It's not as simple as that. You see, the computer doesn't make decisions. It just supplies probability assessments to the corporations in the network.

"It's like using a computer to help you play a game of chess. The computer analyzes the board and then gives you the moves that are most likely to result in victory. You want to win, so you do what the computer suggests. To do otherwise would be patently foolish. And after a while, you realize that you're the redundant part of the process. You're just an appendage of the machine, moving the pieces while it does the thinking. But it's always right, so why would you do anything else?

"The Brainstorm network kept making the right decisions, and kept growing and growing, gaining a majority stake in the world's biggest corporations and institutions, and they in turn profited immensely.

"But these corporations need stability. Things like war and terrorism are disruptive; the quaint notion of a military industrial complex and war profiteering…that's an obsolete paradigm. Brainstorm wants to keep things peaceful. That's why it pays people like me an obscene amount of money to make sure that nothing upsets the apple cart."

Sara shook her head, incredulous. "This is all true?"

"The Brainstorm network exists. A lot of the rest is just supposition, but based on the communications I've received, I don't think it's a stretch to believe that there's an artificial intelligence running the show."

"And that doesn't bother you?"

Fulbright shrugged. "I get paid very well. And besides, it's making all the right decisions. Like I said, we need stability in this world. Believe it or not, I'm one of the good guys."

"You're a psychopath."

"If you say so." The roguish smile hardened, and Fulbright keyed the switch that patched his headset in to the external radio. "Please tell me Sigler is finally dead."

21.

Noise and dust enveloped King as bullets split the air around him, striking the ground directly in his path or zinging harmlessly into the sky. A red tracer round occasionally flashed past, like a laser bolt from a science fiction movie weapon. It seemed impossible that none of the shots had yet found him, and he figured it was only a matter of time before that changed. But he was still alive, still on his feet, and still moving, and as long as he had that, there was still hope.

He kept changing directions every few steps. It increased the distance separating him from his ultimate goal—the cave entrance—but if he ran in a straight line, he would be an easy target. Like his chess piece namesake, King's only advantage was his ability to move in any direction, and he knew it wouldn't be enough to turn the tables on the mysterious attack force.

Behind him, one of the helicopters began powering up, and he knew without looking that both Felice and Sara were aboard—one of them held the key to a weapon that might conceivably unmake the human race, the other held the key to his heart. Part of his mind wanted to wrestle with the puzzle of what had happened, but he pushed away everything that wasn't directly related to figuring out how to survive the next few seconds.

Though it felt like an eternity, it probably took him less than twenty seconds to make the meandering dash across the open area to the cave mouth. He plunged headlong into the darkness, trusting the memory of his earlier explorations to guide him through the impenetrable black. The gunshots ceased almost immediately, but King did not stop running until the cave's mass swallowed up the noise of the departing helicopter. Even then, he kept moving, one hand extended forward to prevent him from smacking headlong into the mass of elephant bones.

He didn't trust the darkness to provide him safety. If the men accompanying Fulbright were the professionals he thought they were, then they would almost certainly have night-vision equipment; they would be able to sneak up on him without betraying their presence with flashlights. But he did have one thing going for him; he knew that he wasn't alone in the cave.

King located the edge of the bone pile and skirted along the perimeter, searching for the path leading to the tusk shrine. There was risk in seeking refuge amidst the zombies; without Felice to command them, they might simply attack as soon as they detected his presence.

His outstretched hand guided him along the wall of bones until he reached the clearing. In the total darkness, he could hear the noise of the zombies, laboring in the dark, perhaps continuing their work of transforming the shrine into a cathedral, or perhaps gnawing on the bones of the dead. He turned to where he thought the center of the clearing was located, and then struck out blindly toward the shrine.

For once, luck was on his side. He found the massive structure almost exactly where he thought it would be. He turned right and circled around to what he hoped was the back side of the shrine—it was impossible to know for certain—and hunkered down to wait.

The wait wasn't nearly as long as he thought it would be.

The commandos did not make a sound as they entered the clearing. But their stealth counted for little when one of them opened up on a target, presumably one of the zombies. That single shot opened the floodgates, and for the next few seconds, gunfire reverberated throughout the spacious cavern. There were at least two different rifles firing—King thought they were M-16s or some variant thereof—interspersed with shouted commands, but then something changed. The frequency of the shots trailed off, and less than a minute later, they ceased altogether, as did the shouts. The only sound that remained was of flesh tearing and bones cracking, only a few meters away.

King kept waiting.

The next sound he heard was of something wet sliding across stone. In his mind's eye, he could see the zombies dragging their victims to the charnel pile. He followed their actions as best he could, and roughly pinpointed the location where the noises stopped. When he heard nothing more, he moved from his hiding place and struck out across the darkness.

Once more, his instincts led him true. His searching hands, and in no small measure, his sense of smell, led him to the heap of decaying bodies that had evidently become a food source for the zombies. Mixed in with the smell of decay, he detected the coppery smell of fresh blood and the odor of recently fired weapons, and after some trial and error, his hands encountered something that wasn't flesh, but rather hard plastic—the butt-stock of an assault weapon. He kept probing until he found what he was really looking for—the dead commando's night vision goggles.

As best he could tell, it was a military standard A/N PVS-14 monocular night optic device. He held it to his right eye and worked the power switch to reset the device and turn it on. After a moment or two, the interior of the cave was revealed to him, rendered in a murky monochrome green.

The zombies had resumed working in the bones, but their ranks had been reduced by three and two of the survivors appeared to be bleeding from wounds to their extremities, wounds that would likely prove fatal in the short term. The floor was stained with blood and littered with shell casings, but King also spied a discarded M-4 carbine. He turned back to the stack of bodies, and wrestled one of the dead commandos out of his load-carrying vest. A quick check showed four full thirty-round magazines in the ammo pouch, along with two fragmentation grenades and a gaudy, oversized Rambo-style combat knife. With the night vision device strapped in place and wearing the vest, he crept past the oblivious zombies, collecting the carbine as he made his way out of the clearing.

He expected, at any moment, to encounter a second assault team, but that did not happen. He made it as far as the cave entrance before spying two figures silhouetted against the opening. He drew back quickly, and then hastened to the far end of the tunnel, a plan already taking shape in his mind.

King knew that eventually they would want to find out why their comrades had failed to report back, but he didn't have time to wait them out. He needed a diversion, something to draw the rest of the team into the cave.

When he reached the edge of the elephant graveyard, he did not circle around as before, but instead climbed onto the piled skeletons, scrambling to the top of the nest of bones that were as thick as tree trunks. From this vantage, he took out one of the grenades, armed it, and hurled it out across the graveyard.

Five seconds later, the cavern resounded with an enormous thump. King felt the bones beneath him ripple with the concussive force, and a few seconds later, a shower of debris rained down on him, but his perch remained more or less stable. He nevertheless kept his head down, and once again waited to see if his plan would work.

It did. Two more commandos wearing night-vision devices entered the tunnel and raced down to investigate the blast.

King decided not to snipe them from his perch. If he failed to kill both men quickly, he would lose the advantage he had created with the diversion. Instead, he let the men pass by, and when they had, he dropped down to the cavern floor and hastened up the tunnel.

From the cavern entrance, he surveyed the dark landscape. A helicopter was parked a hundred meters away, and a single figure, presumably the pilot, lurked nearby, calmly smoking a cigarette. From a distance, the man didn't appear to be wearing night-vision goggles. King crept across the open area, watching to see if the pilot would notice his approach, but the man remained oblivious until it was too late. King clubbed him senseless with the butt of the carbine and left him on the ground alongside the chopper.

It was, King now saw, a Bell 206 JetRanger, one of the most popular commercial helicopters in service. As part of his Special Forces training, King had learned how to fly the military variant—the Kiowa OH-58—and although it had been a few years, once in the pilot's seat, it all came back to him. He started flipping switches and felt a thrill of exhilaration as the turbine engine started powering up.

The lights on the instrument panel flared brightly in his night-vision display, but he kept the device turned on and simply shut his right eye when it was necessary to look at the panel. A minute later, he gave the collective control lever a nudge, and as the rotor blades tilted and started pushing air, the helicopter lightened and lifted off the ground. As soon as it was hovering, he pushed the cyclic forward and the Bell shot ahead, across the floor of the valley.

As his forward velocity increased, the helicopter got more and more lift, and soon was climbing into the night sky. He scanned in all directions, and quickly located the running lights of the first helicopter near the western horizon, already forty or fifty miles away. Without the added weight of passengers, he would be able to push the throttle a little harder and close that gap.

He didn't know what he was going to do when he caught up to them, but by his best estimate, he had about thirty minutes to come up with a plan.

22.

Fulbright's face grew dark as he received the status report from the assault team he'd left behind. Sara's headset wasn't wired into the external comms, but she had no trouble interpreting the message written in his scowl. Not only was Jack still alive, but he was fighting back. She tried, unsuccessfully, to hide her smile.

Fulbright must have noticed because an evil gleam appeared in his eyes. "Patch me through to our contact in the Ethiopian Air Force. There's an unauthorized aircraft out here that they need to know about."

He moved the mic away from his lips and Sara saw that his smile was back. "Your boyfriend should have kept his feet on the ground."

23.

The two ETAF Russian-made Sukhoi Su-25 fighter jets approached from behind King and struck without warning.

Fortunately for him, the pilots had been instructed to engage with guns only. With an equivalent price tag of more than $70,000, the Vympel R-73 infrared guided air-to-air missiles they carried were deemed too costly to be used as a first-strike measure against a slow moving and evidently unarmed helicopter. Absent that consideration, he would have died without even knowing that he was in danger. Instead, the lead plane greeted him with a short burst from its Gryazev-Shipunov GSh-30-2 30 millimeter cannon.

Eighteen of the twenty-one rounds fired in that initial volley arced harmlessly past the JetRanger. Two of the rounds were phosphorous-tipped tracers that lit up the display of King's night-vision device like streaks of lightning. But even as those rounds were flashing by, betraying the presence of hostile aircraft, the other three rounds hit their target. The helicopter shuddered as the projectiles, as thick as flashlight batteries and nearly three times as long, penetrated the aluminum and Lexan airframe. Even though they struck neither flesh nor critical systems, King felt the heat and concussive force on his skin as the rounds passed through the cockpit, far too close for comfort.

King had no idea who was shooting at him, or even what kind of aircraft was involved, but he knew luck alone had saved him. He was an easy target. He hastily reduced the collective pitch and the helicopter immediately dropped almost straight down. More tracers lit up the night, flashing harmlessly overhead. He looked up and saw, blazing like a miniature suns, the engine exhaust of the two attack planes as they flew through the space where he had been only a moment before. The jets arced across the night sky, maneuvering to come around for another pass at him.

The planes' superior speed was both an advantage and a liability. Because they were so much faster than the helicopter, they could attack from almost anywhere, but at the same time that speed would make it very difficult to hit him with cannon-fire. King didn't know why they hadn't simply fired a heat-seeker up his exhaust pipe, but he had no doubt that eventually they would, and then it would all be over. There was, he realized, only one way to survive this.

He kept descending, tilting the cyclic forward and increasing speed in a power dive. The barren landscape, rendered even bleaker in the monochrome night-vision display, rushed up at him. He leveled out less than a hundred feet above the uneven terrain, and began weaving the aircraft back and forth, all the while keeping an eye on the distant moving lights in the sky.

The jets made another attack run, strafing the ground nearby as if he were a stationary target, but King came about and steered under them, well away from danger. The jets broke off and winged skyward, repositioning once again.

King's instincts told him that the gloves were about to come off. His attackers had probably expected him to be easy pickings, but now that he had demonstrated his ability to elude them, they would look for a quick, decisive solution. His mind raced to find anything that would help him survive the next few seconds.

The JetRanger wasn't equipped with any weapon systems. He had the M-4 he'd taken from the cavern, but that wouldn't be much use in a dogfight, even if he had a hand free to use it. He also had one frag grenade.

Maybe... A grin spread across his King's face. It was a crazy plan, but crazy was better than nothing.

He felt certain that the fighter pilots would use missiles on this pass, almost certainly thermal guided missiles, and there was only one way to elude those—make something else even hotter. Unfortunately, that was easier said than done. Since most air-to-air missiles could travel in excess of twice the speed of sound, it would take split second timing.

He watched. He waited. And then, when he saw a bloom of fire under one of the jets, he dropped the grenade out the sliding window, and then hastily pulled up on the collective. The helicopter rose sluggishly, and with each passing second, King knew he was getting closer to the missile now streaking toward him.

But then, he felt the concussion wave of the grenade exploding on the ground a few hundred feet below. For just an instant, the center of the detonation released a burst of intense heat—much hotter than the JetRanger's turbine exhaust. There was a streak of light in his night-vision, the missile flashing by as it homed in on its new target, and then a second later, another concussion.

King was stunned by the success of his plan; it had been a desperate play, and he hadn't really expected it to work, and so hadn't really thought about what would happen next. He had dodged this attack, but what now?   •

The jets veered skyward again. He had fooled the missile, but not the pilots. They knew he was still alive.

And King was out of moves.

Δ Δ Δ

The Sukhoi fighters needed only one more pass. The pilots were relatively inexperienced, but they were learning from their mistakes. The engagement had already lasted longer than either man expected; now it was time to finish it decisively.

The helicopter was descending again, its operator evidently desperate to land before the next missile blew him out of the sky. The pilot of the lead Su-25 decided not to give him that chance. He changed the targeting selector on the missile's guidance system to visual, put the helicopter in the crosshairs, and thumbed the launch button.

The R-73 missile, NATO designation AA-11 Archer, dropped away from the wing and shot through the sky at Mach 2.5. The pilot kept his targeting sight on the fleeing aircraft until, a few seconds later, both the missile and the helicopter exploded in a ball of smoke and flaming debris.

Sigler is dead.

>>>Understood. What is your status?

I'm back in Addis. I have Sara Fogg and Felice Carter with me. Fogg believes that Carter can infect others by some unknown vector. We'll need to keep her isolated.

>>>Transportation will be arranged. Bring the women to the Brainstorm facility.

Are you sure that's a good idea?

>>>Your inquiry is irrelevant. It is the only logical course of action. The vaccine must be developed. The facility has been upgraded to ensure the highest probability of success in accomplishing that goal.

ENDGAME

24.

Unknown Location

See that ball of fire down there? That's your boyfriend.

Fulbright's gleeful pronouncement still echoed in Sara's ears. She had kept a brave face, denying the rogue CIA agent the pleasure of watching her cry. In truth, she hadn't wanted to believe him.

That was, she knew, the first stage of grief: denial.

As an intellectual matter, she did believe him but her heart wasn't ready to deal with it just yet. There would be time for tears later, if she survived.

A Gulfstream V jet had been waiting for them at the private airfield used by the contracted commandos. Still unconscious from the sedative injection, Felice had been buckled into one of the rear seats, while Sara had been allowed to sit where she pleased, but always under Fulbright's watchful eye. How long they flew, she could not say, but when they arrived at their destination, it was mid-morning, and the physical environment did not seem that much different than the place they had just left.

A fit but pale-looking middle-aged man got out of a dark green Range Rover and greeted them as they descended from the jet. His hair was gray, but Sara couldn't tell if he was in his late forties or his early seventies. When he approached and introduced himself, Sara got the impression that it was as much for Fulbright's benefit as for Sara's.

"I'm Graham," he said, affably. "I kind of keep things running around here."

"Just take us to Brainstorm," Fulbright answered impatiently.

"As you like." Graham chuckled then turned to Sara and extended a hand. "A pleasure to make your acquaintance, Miss...?"

Sara narrowed her eyes, appraisingly. Despite his attempt at charm, Graham—was that his first or last name?—had given her no reason to think he was anything but another villain in Brainstorm's employ. "It's 'doctor,' actually. Dr. Sara Fogg."

"Ah, yes. I've heard wonderful things about you, Dr. Fogg. I think you'll be pleased with the research facility here."

"I'll be pleased when I'm not being held prisoner."

Graham inclined his head. "Touché. I do hope that, in time, you will see that benefit of the work you will do here far outstrips the sacrifices you have made."

"I'm not the only one who was sacrificed."

If Graham heard her muttered comment, he chose not to acknowledge it.

Δ Δ Δ

The main house—what Fulbright had called the 'Brainstorm facility'—was a palatial two-story villa that might have been transplanted from the south of France or the Catalina hills of

California. Sara was escorted to a luxurious private room where Graham invited her to "freshen up" and join him for a meal if she was so inclined. A closet full of clothes, ranging in style from dress casual to blue jeans and T-shirts—all of them clothes that she might have purchased for herself, every garment the correct size—was provided, and the bathroom was stocked with her favorite brands of toiletries. Someone had been doing their homework.

No demands were made of her, but there was little question that she was a prisoner. Nevertheless, she took advantage of the chance to shower away the residue of her plunge into the Indian Ocean and the general grime of days spent in the field.

As the hot water cascaded down on her shoulders, she pondered her next move. Things were so much clearer in Jack's world. If you were captured, you would fight back, resist, try to escape or confound your enemy's goals in any way possible. But it was different for her. Yes, she wanted to escape, but she could not afford to so easily dismiss what her captor was attempting. Even if she was being lied to, even if they were secretly trying to turn the discovery into a weapon, the opportunity to do research on the contagion and to find a way to counteract it, was not something she could easily pass up.

It was the best way she had to fight back, resist, and confound her enemy's goals.

The door was locked from the outside, but as soon as she knocked, it popped open revealing an empty hallway. As she stepped into the hall, Graham appeared on the staircase landing, midway down the hall. "This way, Dr. Fogg. Lunch is already set."

The kitchen furnishings, like everything else in the house, were modern, giving the whole place the feel of being on a space station designed by a 1950's science fiction writer. She found Fulbright seated at the oval-shaped glass dining table, pensively eating a sandwich.

"I can only provide light fare right now," Graham apologized.

"But I promise dinner will be superb. I don't get the chance to entertain here very often, so I will be pulling out all the stops."

"I'd hate for you to go to any trouble," Sara replied, with undisguised sarcasm.

Fulbright looked up at her, but said nothing.

"No trouble at all." Graham elected to ignore the venom. "There's no reason your stay here has to be unpleasant."

"That sounds like something he might say." Sara jerked a thumb at the rogue CIA officer. "As a threat," she added.

"Please understand, Dr. Fogg. You have important work to do here. Work that will benefit us all; the entire human race."

Sara settled into a chair and started assembling a sandwich from a plate of assorted cold-cuts and cheeses. "Fine," she said at length. "I'll play along, but I can't have you telling me how to do my research. You need to give me whatever I ask for."

"Within reason, of course."

"First, I want you to stop sedating Felice Carter."

Fulbright looked up sharply. "Weren't you paying attention back there? She can infect people, maybe without even thinking about it. If she feels the least bit threatened…" He snapped his fingers. "Poof, we're mindless drones."

"That's exactly why I need her awake and alert. Just because she's unconscious doesn't mean that her fear response is turned off. She needs to know that she isn't in any danger. I can explain that to her. More importantly, I need to be able to talk to her in order to figure this thing out. The answers are all in her head."

Graham was about to say something, but was interrupted by a buzzing noise from his pocket. He took out a smart phone and looked at the display for a moment, then tapped a few keys and put it away. "I'm sorry. Unrelated business. With respect to your request, Dr. Fogg, I certainly think we can accommodate you if you feel it's that important. I trust you will take all the necessary precautions."

Sara looked at the older man sidelong. She couldn't quite

figure out just what his role was in all of this.

"You need to run this past Brainstorm," Fulbright declared, clearly unhappy about what Sara was demanding.

"And that's the other thing I need," Sara broke in, quickly. "I'm tired of dealing with lackeys...I'm tired of dealing with him." She pointed an accusing finger at Fulbright. "If you want me to do this, I need direct access to Mr. Big himself. I need to be able to talk to Brainstorm."

Graham gave an odd smile. "Done."

△ △ △

After the meal, she was taken to the laboratory facilities, which were she surmised, in a basement level beneath the villa. The lab was accessible only by elevator, and she was pretty sure that it had gone down, not up, but the spacious windowless area could have been almost anywhere.

Graham showed her a computer workstation and logged her in. "This terminal is linked to a pair of Cray supercomputers which you can use for gene sequencing, and any other applications that will help you design a vaccine. And this icon here—" He clicked on a tab on the desktop display—"This allows you to send instant text messages to Brainstorm."

"I don't want to text Brainstorm," Sara countered. "I want to talk to him. Face to face."

"Good luck with that," Fulbright remarked.

"All communications from Brainstorm are via text messages," Graham explained, "but I'll activate the text-to-voice translator. I'm afraid that's about as close as you can get to actually having a conversation with Brainstorm."

Sara stared back at him. "So it's true. Brainstorm is just a big computer—artificial intelligence."

Graham spread his hands equivocally, and then stepped out from behind the workstation. "Dr. Carter is in the isolation room. It's equipped with Level A hazmat protection, if you feel the need for such measures. On the other hand, if you feel that she poses no threat, I'll arrange guest quarters for her later."

"Do that. I've got it from here. I'll let you know if I need anything more."

The two men lingered in the lab a while after she dismissed them, but as far as Sara was concerned, they were already gone. She gave Felice an anti-narcotic injection then sat down and waited for her to stir.

Despite her confident demeanor, she was very worried about Felice's transition from drug induced sleep to wakefulness. Indeed, as the sedative in her bloodstream was bound and rendered inert by the anti-narcotic, Felice came awake as if emerging from a night terror.

"Felice, it's okay." Sara risked physical contact, gently holding Felice's forearm. "You're safe."

Felice's eyes darted back and forth as she tried to take in the unfamiliar surroundings. "Where am I?"

"I wish I knew. But we're safe for now. You need to relax and stay calm. I'll explain everything."

The roving gaze finally settled on Sara's face. "I know you. You're the CDC doctor."

"That's right. I'm Sara. I feel like I know you well, but I guess we only got to meet for a few minutes. A lot has happened since then, and I'll tell you when you're ready to hear it."

"Where's Jack?"

The question caught Sara off guard, and emotion welled up in her throat. After a false start, she managed to croak: "That's part of what I have to tell you."

"Tell me now."

Sara started with Fulbright's act of treachery. She only gave the barest of details about what had happened to Sigler, and it was evident from Felice's reaction that she understood why it was so painful; she had, after all, witnessed their affectionate reunion.

Once Felice understood that they were both being held hostage, Sara turned her attention to the contagion—if a contagion it indeed was. Sara wasn't convinced of that. "We need to understand exactly how this…effect…is being spread. I'm thinking that maybe it's linked to a pheromone."

Felice shook her head. "Sara, I need to tell you a story; a story about elephants."

25.

Somewhere over Africa

A black wraith-like shape tore through the sky high above the dark continent. Anyone looking skyward would have immediately recognized the tiny speck as an aircraft by the long contrail—the product of water vapor in the jet exhaust instantly freezing into ice crystals high in the stratosphere—but such sights were common almost everywhere in the world. Anyone watching a radar display would have seen absolutely nothing. The stealth transport plane, code-named Crescent because of its unique, radar-scattering half-moon profile, was for practical purposes, invisible.

King sat in Crescent's communication center, just aft of the cockpit, where two pilots from the USAF Nighthawks special operations wing, were waiting for their next destination. Unfortunately, King didn't yet know what that would be.

One of the two computer screens on the workstation showed photographic imagery from a satellite in a geostationary orbit above northern Africa. Deep Blue had accessed the feed from the National Reconnaissance Office and cued it up to approximately the moment where King's helicopter had been shot down by a missile from one of the Ethiopian fighter jets. King wasn't interested in the crash though; he already knew how that ended.

With the realization that he would not be able to fool another missile attack, King did the only thing he could: he cut the engine and let the helicopter fall from the sky. The plunge was only about sixty feet, and the helicopter was engineered to withstand hard landings, but even so, the impact was like getting hit by a bus. Battered, bruised, but thankfully not broken, he had half-fallen out of the crumpled cockpit and taken off across the scrubland in search of cover. A few moments later, a second missile had homed in on the helicopter and blown it to smithereens. The concussion wave had sent him tumbling, adding a few more bruises, but the ploy had worked. The Sukhoi fighters had turned for home, satisfied that, even if he had survived, the elements would finish him off.

Fortunately, King had his Chess Team phone. Rescue, in the form of Crescent, traveling halfway around the world at Mach 2, had arrived a few hours later. Now, he was tracking the other helicopter, the one that had borne Sara and Felice Carter away.

"That's where they landed in Addis Ababa," Deep Blue observed from Chess Team headquarters in New Hampshire. His face was visible on the second computer screen and his voice was a tinny electronic reproduction in King's headphones. "That compound belongs to Alpha Dog Solutions, a private security firm that's doing counter-terrorism operations under contract for the CIA."

"Sara told me that Fulbright might be a CIA officer."

"I couldn't verify that. If he really is with the Company, then he's probably NOC, and information on that is too closely guarded for me to root out with just a discreet inquiry." The acronym stood for "non-official cover" and was reserved for intelligence operatives working deep undercover espionage missions. "Or it could just be an alias," Deep Blue added.

King rubbed his eyes. Despite his ability to thrive under the worst conditions, fatigue was finally starting to take its toll. "What else do we know about Alpha Dog? Do they have other clients?"

"In that region, they also do site security for a number of petroleum companies. Curiously enough, it looks like they received several payments, all from different clients and all in the last three days. If I had to guess, I'd say someone was trying to hide the actual size of a very large payoff by splitting it up... Oh."

"What?"

"The men who attacked you on the road from the airport, when you first arrived, were Alpha Dog contractors, not Gen-Y."

"I guess they knew I'd make trouble, and wanted me out of the way." King glanced back at the satellite feed, where a group of tiny figures moved between the now stationary helicopter and a small private jet. A few frames later, the jet taxied for take-off. "Do we know who owns the jet?"

Deep Blue consulted his own computer screen. "A shell company. I'm starting to get the sense that someone is trying very hard to cover their tracks."

"So what do we know for sure? This guy, Fulbright, was able to call out the CDC through official channels; let's assume that means he really does work in some government agency, but he's gone rogue. His real employer has almost unlimited resources, and the ability to channel money through a number of different corporations. And let's not forget, somehow they were keeping an eye on what Manifold was up to. They knew what Felice Carter brought back from the elephant graveyard almost from the start."

"That kind of reach takes a lot of money; more money than multinational corporations, more money than most governments." Deep Blue's eyebrows drew together in a perplexed frown. "When I was in office, there was chatter about a… I guess you could call it a 'metacorporation'—an entity that was secretly insinuating itself into other corporations, the really big multinationals, using shell companies and phony proxies to take over, essentially creating a gigantic global monopoly."

"How would you keep something like that off the radar?"

"Logistically, it would be almost impossible. One person couldn't run something so complex, and if you had a board of directors…well, eventually someone would slip up, or get greedy and break away…or they would just make bad decisions and it would all come unglued. But that never seemed to happen. There were rumors that the whole thing might be controlled from cyberspace by a sentient computer network. Artificial intelligence would be one explanation for the level of control that's been exhibited."

King shook his head. Global conspiracies were the last thing on his mind right now. "What does any of this have to do with Sara? Or with what Felice discovered in that cave?"

"If it involves bioweapons research, then I can think of at least one nightmare scenario. Radical depopulation. Selective reduction of undesirable elements in the population as a way of increasing control and bringing about economic stability."

King thought about what he had witnessed in the cavern. "So, give the 'desirable' people the vaccine, and then turn the rest into zombies. A drone workforce that never complains, never rises up in revolt, and will defend you without question."

Deep Blue nodded. "That's exactly how a computer would reason. The economically disadvantaged represent a constant source of social instability. From ancient times, kings and emperors controlled the masses with distractions—gladiatorial games, circuses, daytime talk shows—but now there's the potential to simply switch off the part of the human brain that causes discontent."

"They already have the way to throw the switch. They just don't have a vaccine for the 'desirables.' That's what they need

Sara for." King took a deep breath. "Do we know where they took her?"

"I've tracked the plane ahead for six hours. It looks like they're still in Africa—Algeria, to be precise."

King's screen showed an overhead view of a plane sitting at the end of a runway, and a road that connected the airstrip to a large fenced compound nearby. There were no other roads or buildings anywhere in the featureless brown landscape.

"I can't find any records connected to that property," Deep Blue continued. "In fact, according to the maps, it's supposed to be a national park."

"Money and influence. Bribe the right official, and do as you please." King clicked on a button to zoom in on the compound. "It doesn't appear to be built-up."

"I'll have the Crescent deploy our UAV and recon the area so we can determine how well defended it is. I'm afraid the rest of the team is unavailable and—"

"And the rest of the U.S. military is off limits to us now that we're black, I know," King said. "Tell me again why we went underground?"

But King knew why. The less people that knew about the...evils Chess Team faced, the better off the world would be. And it was just as likely that more military would get in his way, or turn this into an international incident, which wouldn't be a good thing for a fledgling black op, especially one directed by a former U.S. President.

"I could hire some mercenaries," Deep Blue said.

King laughed, but when Deep Blue didn't join him, he asked, "You're serious?"

"We have a budget for it now."

King had some military friends that had become mercs. They were trustworthy, and a few extra guns would be nice, but ultimately, this had to be a solo mission for one very important reason. "This contagion, whatever it is, seems to be triggered specifically by a threat to Felice's safety. If we raid the compound, it'll probably scare the hell out of her, and believe me, you don't want that to happen."

26.

Brainstorm facility, Algeria

"What is the status of your research?"

Sara jumped at the sound of the electronically produced voice. After hours of conversing with Felice in a tone so low it was almost a whisper, the computerized speech was almost ear-splitting. "Is that you Brainstorm?"

"Affirmative. What is the status of your research? You have not yet drawn blood or tissue samples for analysis. How do you intend to conduct research and develop a vaccine without collecting specimens for study?"

Sara detected a very uncomputer-like note of sarcasm in the utterance. It was however the truth. She had not taken a single sample nor performed even one diagnostic test. She had simply listened as Felice recounted a bizarre tale of past lives and what sounded very much like spirit possession. Sara didn't believe in reincarnation or ghostly hauntings, but she had come up with an alternative theory.

She put her hands on her hips. She didn't know if Brainstorm had eyes as well as ears in the room, but she wanted him...or maybe it...to know she was defiant. "If you're such a genius, why don't you do it yourself?"

"Are you stating that you no longer wish to be involved in the research?"

Sara sighed. So much for defiance. "Look Braniac, this is what I do and I'm very good at it. So give me some time and space. Nagging me won't make things happen any faster."

"There is a 69.4% probability that you are purposefully delaying. It would not be in your best interests to attempt to prolong this process as an act of resistance. Your survival is contingent upon your usefulness. This is also true for your patient. The research can be conducted equally as well using samples taken post-mortem."

Sara wanted to scream, *Don't you get it? There isn't going to be a vaccine. Not for this. Kill her, and you kill the whole human race*! But revealing her suspicions about the "contagion" to a soulless computer was probably a very bad idea. She had seen too many science fiction movies where sentient computers decided that the world would be better off without their human creators. If Brainstorm realized the true potential of what Felice had discovered, then there was no telling how that might affect its grand scheme.

"Fine," she said, evincing defeat. "I'll take some blood samples if it will make you happy."

At least, she thought, *I know it's not eavesdropping on us.* Indeed, if Brainstorm had been listening in, it would already know that she wasn't actually stalling, and it would know the sheer futility of trying to develop a vaccine.

As Felice had related the story of her shared memory with an ancient primate female she called "Old Mother," Sara had wracked her brain to come up with a rational explanation for what had happened to the woman.

Most troubling was the nearly instantaneous nature of the reactions. Even the most virulent contagions required several hours incubation time before a patient became symptomatic. But Felice had been overcome almost from the moment she touched the Old Mother's skull. And Jack had described how the man attacking Felice had been changed into a mindless zombie "just like that." Her pheromone theory couldn't account for that, any more than the idea that it was all the result of a viral infection.

There was only one force in the universe that had been proven to cause instantaneous sympathetic action across distances of both space and time; a force known as quantum entanglement.

Felice's memories of the Old Mother verified Manifold's notion that exposure to a particular retrovirus had been the pivotal event in the evolution of human consciousness. It had rewritten the Australopithecine female's genetic code, and made that newly awakened consciousness a heritable trait, which had started the snowball rolling. Consciousness had been passed along to all of her offspring as a genetic trait, not because of continued exposure to the original retrovirus. That contagion had been out of the picture long before the Old Mother's entombment in the elephant graveyard, which meant that there had to be another explanation for what had happened to Felice.

Quantum entanglement described a connection between subatomic particles separated by vast distances; when two particles interact and are subsequently separated, a change to one of the particles had an effect on the other. By its very nature, the replication of the DNA molecule, within each cell in a body, and from one generation to the next, facilitated quantum interaction on a staggering scale. If her hypothesis was correct, then every human on the planet was part of the tangle.

It was one possible explanation for the oft-described phenomenon where one of a set of identical twins reported seeing or feeling things that were happening to the other. Indeed, because quantum entanglement was not limited by temporal distance, the effect was probably the cause of almost everything that fell under the umbrella of the paranormal, from psychic visions to past-life experiences, alien abductions to religious visitations. Somehow, the quantum wires got crossed up and the brain tuned into something experienced by someone else in another place or time.

If Sara was correct, it was the real cause of what had happened, both to Felice and to her unlucky co-workers. Felice had connected with the Old Mother, and that had somehow loosened the wires connecting the section of the genome responsible for human sentience. The other Nexus researchers had come unplugged, and it seemed that, as part of some instinctive defense mechanism, Felice could do the same to others. And that was what really frightened Sara.

If Brainstorm followed through on its threat to simply kill Felice, there was no telling how far the ripples would spread. Felice was linked to the Old Mother, and the Old Mother was the source of human consciousness. Destroying that connection might conceivably mean the instantaneous end of humanity; an entire world of people, turned to zombie-apes in the blink of an eye.

Brainstorm's probability assessment was wrong; she wasn't stalling. In truth, there was nothing she could do.

Brainstorm wasn't finished. "In order to expedite your research, access to the guest level had been rescinded."

"Are you saying we can't leave this room?"

"Affirmative. How you choose to employ your time is at your discretion. However, results are required. You will be supervised from this point forward. Furthermore, your progress will be reviewed in thirty-six hours. If it is determined that you are unable or unwilling to achieve the desired results, you will be terminated."

Thirty-six hours, Sara thought. That was how long she had left to live. And maybe all the time left for the human race.

27.

King hung suspended beneath the fluttering cells of a black stealth-parachute, falling gently out of the African night sky. He had decided to infiltrate the remote compound using a high-altitude, high-opening (HAHO) jump, instead of the high-altitude, low-opening (HALO) jump that Chess Team usually favored, for the simple reason that HAHO would afford ample opportunity to adjust his plan as circumstances on the ground dictated. As King glided across the sky, with the prevailing wind at his back, and now some sixty horizontal miles from where he'd left a perfectly good airplane, he watched the real-time video feed, supplied by the Predator drone that was presently circling the target, and relayed to the display in his night-vision goggles.

For all he could tell, the compound might have been abandoned. There was no sign of a security force. In fact, more than twelve hours of surveillance by the team's personal satellite and UAV had shown no exterior activity whatsoever. In a way, that made a lot of sense. If Deep Blue's idea about a global metacorporation was anywhere close to the truth, then absolute secrecy would be imperative. The more people that knew about something—whether mercenaries hired to protect it or food service workers brought in to feed everyone—the more chance there was for that cloak of secrecy to slip away.

King just hoped that Deep Blue was wrong about the whole thing being run by a sentient supercomputer; the last thing he wanted was to run up against an army of killer robots.

Still, if it came to that, he was ready. Slung from one shoulder was a FN Herstal SCAR H heavy combat assault rifle, outfitted with the FN40GL enhanced grenade launching module. His load-carrying vest held nine spare 20 round magazines of 7.62 X 51 mm ammunition for the rifle, along with five M433 high-explosive dual-purpose grenades and five M576 "Beehive" buckshot rounds, either of which could be used in the FN40GL. For more intimate acts of violence, he also carried a SiG P220 Combat pistol outfitted with a suppressor, and a black KA-BAR straight-edge knife. He also carried a satchel full of C-4 and detonator caps, useful for everything from door breaching to large scale demolitions.

The prodigious weight of his combat load was partially offset by the switch from the traditional Kevlar and porcelain plate body armor, to an experimental dilatant liquid body armor suit, which he wore under his black BDUs. The garment, which looked and felt like a neoprene wetsuit, utilized a shear thickening fluid, sandwiched between two layers of durable Kevlar fabric. When a ballistic projectile struck the garment, the fluid instantly became rigid, preventing penetration and dispersing the energy of impact, but under normal circumstances, it allowed a full range of movement and relatively little discomfort to the wearer. King also sported a black hockey helmet, which had been augmented with dilatant filled pads, to afford protection from both bullets and impact trauma.

It was never possible to be prepared for everything, but King didn't think there was much that his unknown enemy would be able to throw at him that he couldn't deal with, even killer robots.

He checked the UAV feed one last time and then switched

his goggles back to night-vision mode. The display didn't change that much. He was very close. He steered his chute into a corkscrew spiral and a few seconds later pulled hard on the toggle wires, flaring the chute to drop feather light onto the roof of the villa.

Despite Deep Blue's best efforts, King knew absolutely nothing about what lay just below his feet. The house had been heavily insulated, resisting every form of remote sensor scan, and because it wasn't supposed to exist, there were no architectural blueprints on record. King was going to have to search the house, room by room.

He chose to make his entry through a second-story window on the west end of the house. He rigged up a hasty rope belay, with one end tied around a vent pipe on the roof, and lowered himself down the side of the house, just to the right of the enormous opening. The curtains were drawn on the other side of the glass, but his goggles did not detect even a trace of light from beyond.

King scanned the glass visually and then swept it with a portable RF detector. The latter device was designed to pick up even the smallest fluctuations in the ambient electrical field, such as might come from alarm sensors and security cameras, but the needle on the meter did not quiver. Cautious nevertheless, he tapped the tempered pane with the hilt of his KA-BAR until it finally cracked. He carefully pulled away the broken window in large sections, pushing them into the house's interior rather than letting them fall to the ground outside, and then crawled through.

The space beyond was enormous, and King soon realized that it was the sitting area for what was essentially a small apartment, or perhaps a guest suite. As expected, the room was unoccupied. In fact, it was completely devoid of furnishings and looked as if it had never been used. But the sensitive optics of his night-vision device did reveal a strip of bright light streaming in from under the exit. He switched off the night vision, and pushed the eyepiece up onto his helmet, where it would continue to transmit live video to Deep Blue. With his P220 at the ready, he eased the door open.

Beyond lay an empty hallway, illuminated by a single overhead light, blazing from a decorative fixture. Three doors, similar to the one through which he had just passed, lined the hall before it opened up onto a broad staircase landing. King stole forward and opened the next door down the line.

As soon as he entered, he knew that Sara had been in this room. He could smell the distinctive fragrance of her favorite soap and hair care products. Because of her SDD, Sara had to be very picky about perfumes and other scents in her bath products, and that unique combination of organic ingredients was unmistakable. But his excitement was short-lived; Sara might have been here earlier, but now she was gone.

He crept back into the hallway and tried the next door.

Here too there were the distinctive odors of human occupation, though none as evocative as Sara's fragrance. But unlike the other suites, this room's inhabitant was still there. A gray-haired Caucasian man sat calmly on a sofa in the front room, intently studying the display on a smartphone and evidently oblivious to the intrusion.

King checked his impulse to simply dispatch the man then and there, and instead cleared his throat. The man looked up and what little color there was in his pale face drained away.

"Put the phone down and keep your hands where I can see them," King instructed in a level voice

The man complied without saying a word.

"Very good. You get to live a little longer. Now, who the hell are you?"

"It seems like I should be asking you that question."

King triggered a silenced round and a neat hole appeared in the upholstery, three inches to the right of the man's shoulder. "Try again."

The corner of the man's mouth twitched into something

that might have been a smile. "I see your point. The name's Graham."

"Better. Elaborate a little."

Graham spread his raised hands a little wide, gesturing at his surroundings. "This is my house."

King cocked his head sideways. "See, that just makes me want to kill you even more. But as long as you keep answering truthfully, you'll keep breathing. Now, here's the important question, and don't screw this one up. Where can I find Sara Fogg?"

"She's working in the research laboratory. It's in the sub-basement, but you won't be able to access it." Graham thought a moment, and then added. "I can take you there."

There was a scratch of static in King's ear as Deep Blue initiated contact. "King, I've run a facial recognition program on him and matched him to a file photo that's almost thirty years old. His name really is Graham—Graham Brown. He's American, born in New Jersey. Made a small fortune gambling, and then made an even bigger fortune on the stock market. He seems to have had an uncanny ability to predict trends, even in a down market. He's also a notorious recluse, and pretty much vanished from public life in the 1980's."

"Roger," King answered, subvocalizing. He then waved the P220 in Graham's direction. "Graham...Brown is it?"

The other man's eye twitched ever so slightly, but that was the only indication of dismay at having been correctly identified.

"You must have been a hell of a poker player back in the day," King continued. "But if you're trying to bluff me now, it will cost you everything."

"I never played poker. It's a game of deceit. I prefer to deal in mathematical probabilities. But I do always play to win...Mr. Sigler."

It was King's turn to hide his dismay. "Cards on the table, then. You've tried very hard to have me killed Graham, and that makes me a little cranky. So, take me to Sara and don't do anything stupid."

"As you wish. I'm going to stand up now." Graham waited a beat, and then lowered his hands in order to push himself up from the sofa.

"Is there anyone else here?"

"Mr. Fulbright—I believe you know him—is in a room down the hall. Miss Carter is in the laboratory with Dr. Fogg." As an afterthought, he added: "And the flight crew for my Gulfstream is in the coach house."

"None of your Alpha Dog mercenaries running around?"

Graham offered a bitter smile. "No, more's the pity. I prefer not to have dogs in the house, but I can see that perhaps it would have been a good idea."

King gestured with the gun. "Lead the way."

Graham eased past King and moved to the exit. As he followed, King keyed his mic. "Anything else you can tell me about this guy?"

"Nothing current," Deep Blue answered. "But his disappearance coincides with the emergence of the metacorporation. It's conceivable that he's responsible for creating the AI that's behind it all."

King offered a noncommittal grunt but said nothing more as he followed the silver-haired man down the hall to the staircase landing. They descended in silence and made their way to the elevator foyer where Graham pressed a button to summon the car. As the double doors slid aside, King made a point of holding the P220 to the base of Graham's neck.

They filed into the empty car where Graham pushed a button marked SB1. King noted that there was also an SB2. "What's on the bottom floor?"

"That's the computer room," Graham answered, disinterestedly. "It's easier to keep them cool down there."

King made a mental note of that. He also noted that, despite Graham's earlier assertion that King would be unable to access the subbasement without his help, there hadn't been any visible security measures.

The brief vertical journey ended and the doors slid open to reveal a large room rendered in sterile white and stainless steel. Graham raised his hands and waited for a signal from King. "I did what you asked, Mr. Sigler. Are you going to kill me now?"

"Don't tempt me. Out. Take me to Sara."

Graham nodded slowly. "Right this way."

The silver-haired man took a step out of the elevator, and then suddenly threw himself to the right, out of King's line of sight. King squeezed off a round, but was a fraction of a second too slow. And even as the pistol twitched in his hands, he realized that Graham had told another lie. Fulbright wasn't sequestered in a room on the second floor; he was standing twenty feet away, aiming a pistol at the elevator's sole remaining occupant.

Before King could do anything to stop him, he fired.

28.

His liquid body armor stopped Fulbright's bullet from piercing his heart, but the impact was like getting hit in the chest with a baseball bat. King staggered back, rebounding off the wall of the elevator car as Fulbright fired again and again.

The rogue CIA agent was trying for a headshot.

King twisted to the side, and blindly squeezed off a volley from the P220. Fulbright was already gone. Struggling to breathe past the pain in his chest, King pushed off the elevator wall and stormed out, hoping to catch his foe off guard.

Instead, he found Fulbright standing behind Sara, his smoking pistol held against her cheek. "You know how this works, Sigler. I don't give a shit whether you live or die, so you can trust me when I say that the only way you and your girlfriend are going to get out this alive, is if you put down your weapons. But if they don't hit the floor in about five seconds, I promise I will pull this trigger."

King's eyes narrowed as he studied Fulbright across the distance. "Five seconds? One Mississippi…"

"What the hell are you doing?"

King fired the P220.

The .45 caliber ACP round whispered past the suppressor

and plowed into the barely exposed side of Fulbright's head. The CIA man spun away, the pistol falling unused from his nerveless grip.

Sara gaped at King in disbelief. "Nice shooting."

"Thanks. Where's Graham?"

Sara glanced around, but the silver-haired man was gone. Then she was in his arms, unable to hold back the tears. "He said you were dead, but I never believed it. I knew you'd come for me."

He hugged her tight. "Not even God could stop me. Okay, well maybe God, but—"

"It is you!" This incredulous exclamation was from another female voice, and King glanced up to find Felice standing in a few steps behind them. "You sure know how to make an entrance."

King gave her a tight smile. "I know how to make a pretty good exit, too. Come on. Let's get out of here."

Felice nodded eagerly and strode toward the elevator doors. Sara seemed unwilling to let go of him, but he gently loosened her grip while still holding her hand in his. "Let's get you home, Dr. Fogg."

But suddenly his legs were swept from beneath him and fell backward, crashing heavily onto the floor. The impact sent a wave of pain through his body, aggravating a host of scrapes and bruises that had not yet begun to heal, and for a moment, he could only lay motionless, struggling to breathe. That moment was long enough for his attacker to gain the upper hand.

A hideous specter materialized above him; a familiar face—Fulbright's face—on one side, and on the other, a swollen mass of destroyed flesh, weeping blood and serous fluid. His hands sought out King's throat and closed, shutting off the flow of blood to King's brain and the exchange of air to his lungs.

King clawed at Fulbright's choke hold, but could not gain an iota of relief. Dark spots started to swim across his vision, but through the descending night, he saw Sara hammering at the rogue agent's face with her fists in a desperate effort to free King. Nothing worked. Fulbright was almost certainly mortally wounded, certainly suffering incomprehensible pain, but none of that mattered. There was no trace of sanity to be found in his remaining eye, but the force empowering his grip was singular in nature. He wanted King dead, and nothing would prevent that.

He let go of Fulbright's stranglehold and with fumbling fingers, found the hilt of his KA-BAR. Desperately, he slid the blade from its sheath and stabbed out blindly. The knife struck something hard and then twisted out his grip, as King felt his consciousness start to go.

"Stop!"

The commanding voice was barely audible through the roaring in King's ears, but miraculously the darkness began to lift. He drew in a painful breath, welcoming the restored flow of blood to his brain, and struggled to sit up.

Fulbright squatted nearby, his one good eye gazing blankly into space. His injuries continued to bleed, including a new one just below his collarbone, where the hilt of King's KA-BAR protruded, but he seemed unaware of any of it. Covered in blood, he looked almost exactly like....

King turned to meet Felice's gaze and understood in an instant what had happened, what she had done. He searched her eyes, but saw no trace of the guilt or despair that had marked her earlier. She had found some untapped reservoir of strength; the strength to do what needed to be done, and to make an ability out of her liability.

She was probably more dangerous than ever before.

"Thank you," he croaked.

Felice just nodded.

Sara helped him up and held onto him as they moved to the elevator doors. Sara pushed the button calling the car, but nothing happened. The button didn't light up and there was no sound of machinery in the emptiness beyond.

"Graham," King said. "He must have shut them off to strand us down here."

"Or it's Brainstorm," Sara replied.

King cast an inquisitive glance her way and listened intently as she quickly recounted what Fulbright had told her about Brainstorm and her own experiences with the disembodied electronic voice. As she related her suspicions about Brainstorm being a sentient computer, King recalled Deep Blue's metacorporation conspiracy theory, and then he remembered something Graham had told him: subbasement level two was the computer room.

Surely it can't be that easy, King thought.

He was right.

"King, do you read?" Deep Blue's voice scratched in his ears. He sounded a little more frantic than usual.

He keyed his mic. "This is King. Send it."

"I've just detected a massive cruise missile launch, targeted at your coordinates."

"Missiles? Whose?"

"Ours. They were launched from a naval missile frigate. I'm still trying to identify the boat and figure out who ordered the strike, but there are Tomahawks inbound. You've got about ten minutes to get out of there."

"Easier said than done." He released the mic key and quickly relayed the bad news to the others.

Sara's eyes widened, and then she abruptly crossed the room and took a seat in front of a computer desk. "Brainstorm, are you there?" When no answer came, she leaned over the keyboard and tapped out a message.

A moment later, an electronic voice filled the room. "What is your request, Dr. Fogg?"

"Are you responsible for the missiles that are heading here?"

"I am."

"How did you manage that?" King asked, not knowing

whether Brainstorm would respond to him. "Did you hack into the Defense Department?"

"It was not necessary to infiltrate that computer network. I merely sent a priority message to the United States military Central Command, authenticated with Fulbright's credentials, stating that this location is a secret terrorist training camp."

"Why did you do that?" Sara asked, a hint of desperation in her voice.

"He's just covering his tracks," King supplied.

"You are only partially correct, Mr. Sigler. I am also ensuring that you do not survive to further compromise my activities. There is a 72.5% probability that you will make destroying the Brainstorm network a priority, if you are permitted to live."

"There's no 'probable' about it." King said. "I am going to take you apart."

"That is unlikely. The probability that you will survive the missile strike is only 23.2%."

"Brainstorm, you can't do this," Sara pleaded. "You can't...you must not allow Felice to be killed."

"Please explain."

"You already know that Felice was affected by something in that cave, and you know what she can do now, right?"

"Anecdotal reports have been received and evaluated. There is evidence to suggest that Miss Carter is linked to incidences of evolutionary regression. The destruction of the facility will eliminate that threat."

"No it won't. Felice isn't just a carrier of some virus. Her consciousness is quantum entangled with that of the entire human race. If you kill her, it will cause evolutionary regression on a global scale. You'll be responsible for the downfall of humanity."

King searched Sara's eyes and saw that she was deadly serious.

"You are mistaken," Brainstorm replied.

King thought it odd that there was no calculation of

probabilities; Brainstorm was exhibiting the very human tendency of denial. "She's not," he declared. "And you know it. You have to stop this. If Felice dies, humanity dies, and who will you rule over then?"

"That is a chance I will have to take. Good-bye."

29.

Sara continued pleading with Brainstorm, but there was no answer and King knew that salvation would not come from that quarter. He opened a line to Deep Blue. "How long have we got?"

"Estimated time to target is six minutes, thirty seconds... mark."

"I don't suppose you can ask the navy to self-destruct those missiles. You know, maybe say 'pretty-please.'" He tried to sound lighthearted, but he was beginning to worry. In the past, the only people who would miss his passing were the team, who shared the risk and understood it and his mother, who he now realized may or may not have cared about his welfare after all. But now there was Fiona, whose parents died when she was young and whose grandmother was killed in front of her during the attack on the Siletz reservation. She'd put on a tough-girl routine when he left, but he knew his death would affect her profoundly. He'd considered retiring from the field for her, but she'd actually convinced him to stay active. "If you don't fight," she'd said, "the world would be a bad place to live." So here he was fighting, and, it seemed, about to make Fiona regret that little speech.

"You know I can't." Deep Blue sounded distraught. He knew the stakes for King were higher than ever. "Believe me, I'm trying everything. Director Boucher is working the official channels for us and Aleman is trying to hack his way in, disable the missiles, or change their trajectories."

Dominick Boucher was the director of the CIA, Deep Blue's friend and confidant, and the one man who knew everything about Chess Team's new black ops gig. After all, he's the one who set it up. Lewis Aleman was the team's genius techie. An injury took him out of the field, but he's been waging cyber war for the team since. If anyone could take care of the missiles it was them, but stopping several missiles midflight was no easy task, especially when some of the people in danger don't officially exist.

"I know you'll do your best. I'm gonna sign off now. If you don't hear from me in seven minutes…well, you know."

He severed the connection and then turned to Sara and Felice. "Graham was down here with us. Now he's gone. There has to be another way out. Find it."

Sara immediately pointed to a door set against one wall. "I thought that might be a closet, but it's locked."

"I have a key." King loaded a Beehive shell into the SCAR's FN40GL attachment, and took aim at the doorknob. The gun thundered and the entire lock mechanism disintegrated in a cloud of smoke and metal. The door swung back to reveal a landing with a stairs going both up and down. "Go!"

They hastened up the dark stairwell and emerged a few moments later in the elevator foyer on the first floor of the villa. In the distance, there was the roar of a jet engine; not incoming cruise missiles, but the Gulfstream V taking off, presumably with Graham on board.

Sara steered them toward the front door, and they ran from the house, across the courtyard, and through the gate out into the desert. They were still running when the explosions began.

EPILOGUE

Afar District, Ethiopia—One week later

The Old Mother made one more journey to the elephant graveyard.

Felice had spent the week resting and recuperating from injuries she hadn't even realized she'd suffered. Her deepest wounds of course were not physical in nature, and some of them were only now manifesting themselves in the form of chronic insomnia and panic attacks. She had been referred to a specialist in treating post traumatic stress disorder, but deep down she felt there was more to it than that. She knew that she carried within her the ability to undo hundreds of thousands of years of human evolution—to utterly destroy human civilization.

That was a lot for one person to carry.

Good thing that I'm not just one person, she thought. *There's two of us in here.*

But how much longer would that last? The Old Mother's memories were a source of comfort and strength to her, but sometimes she felt that her connection to the past was slipping. She thought about Sara's theory of quantum entanglement; it was as good an explanation as any other she'd entertained. Was it possible to become disentangled?

She hoped so.

"We're just about ready," Jack Sigler announced.

Distracted from her thoughts, she glanced over to where Sigler and Sara were gazing out across the floor of the Rift Valley, to the cave entrance leading into the elephant graveyard, and then went over to join them. Sigler was hunched over a small laptop computer, holding a small joystick controller. The computer display showed the interior of the cave, and when he adjusted the stick, the image on the screen moved.

But nothing else moved in the elephant graveyard. There was no sign of her former co-workers; the men and women who had been transformed into mindless drones were nowhere to be found. Even though she knew in her heart that she was in no way responsible for what had happened to the Nexus team, Felice felt a pang of guilt whenever she thought about them. She hoped that they had at last found peace.

"Coming out now," Sigler announced.

Felice looked to the cave exit, about a hundred yards away, and saw what looked like a miniature bulldozer come rolling out of the opening.

Sigler called it "the Wolverine." The remote controlled military utility robot moved around on tracked wheels, like a battle tank or bulldozer, and was equipped with several surveillance cameras and a powerful manipulator arm that could lift almost two hundred pounds. The Wolverine was primarily used by the military for explosive ordinance removal, but Sigler had used it for almost exactly the opposite purpose.

"Do we really have to do this?" she asked, not for the first time.

Sara nodded grimly. "We can't be sure that the cave doesn't contain some form of the virus that Manifold and Brainstorm were looking for, and we can't take the chance that it might be inadvertently released."

"I know you're right, but I can't help but think about Moses, and his dream to use the ivory in the cave to make Africa a better place."

"It was a noble idea," Sigler said. "But if history has taught us anything, it's that the discovery of some new source of wealth almost never makes things better. Look how quickly his dream was perverted by those rebel fighters."

"And of course, every single one of those elephant carcasses is a potential source of the contagion," Sara added. "To say nothing of the possibility of further quantum contamination."

Felice sighed. "I know that you're both right. But what's the answer? If we can't use something like this to make the world a better place, what's left?"

"You focus on what you've already got," Sigler answered. "Use your skills, your strengths, your passions…that's all any of us can do."

Felice considered this. With everything that had happened, she had lost sight of the simple fact that she was a scientist. Her interest in genetics had grown from a childhood dream of discovering a cure for cancer. Maybe it was time to return to that dream.

Sigler steered the Wolverine across the open expanse and drove it up the ramp of the waiting CH-47 Chinook helicopter that had brought them here. He closed the laptop and tucked in under one arm. "Time to go."

Δ Δ Δ

The twin-rotors lifted the massive Chinook into the sky above the Great Rift Valley and the site of the elephant graveyard. The helicopter circled the area, gaining vertical distance with each pass, until the pilot called back to let King know that they had reached the desired altitude.

King flipped off the red safety cap on the remote triggering device, and then took Felice's hand and placed her finger on the switch. "Would you like to do the honors?"

He could see the hesitation in her eyes. Even though the cave had been the source of unimaginable horrors for her, the uncertainty of what might happen next probably seemed even more terrifying. But King knew well that the first step toward healing was to get some closure.

He nodded to her. "Whenever you're ready."

She smiled weakly, and then pressed the switch.

The device sent out a radio signal that was picked up instantly by a receiver unit on the ground. The receiver in turn sent a small electrical charge surging through several hundred feet of copper wire that disappeared into the cave opening. That charge detonated a small conventional explosive, which scattered a cloud of powdered aluminum high above the maze of elephant skeletons.

A fraction of a second later, the fuel-saturated air ignited.

The thermobaric bomb transformed the elephant graveyard into a miniature sun. The bones and ivory teeth of ancient elephants, crushed to dust by the initial blast front, were subsequently incinerated in a firestorm that exceeded 5,000° Fahrenheit. The force of the explosion hammered into the domed ceiling, opening enormous cracks in the stone. An instant later, the vacuum created by rapid cooling of the scorched air, caused the entire cavern to implode.

From high above, King watched a cloud of dust rising, the result of the shockwave traveling through hundreds of feet of rock. When it cleared, a new crater was visible on the landscape of the Great Rift Valley.

The elephant graveyard had ceased to exist.

>>>Your services are required, General.

I didn't think I'd hear from you again.

>>>The Brainstorm network remains operational.

Sure. I just thought you would be keeping a low profile. At least until some of the heat dies down.

>>>Recent events have not compromised operational efficiency.

Maybe not for you. But I need to be very discreet. Everyone is under suspicion now.

>>>There is no cause for concern. Key network personnel have been positioned to minimize the consequences of this investigation. However, no external action is demanded of you, General.

What then?

>>>Information about the man who caused the recent disruption. I want to know everything about Jack Sigler.

Sigler? I didn't realize he was behind all this. It makes sense now.

>>>You are familiar with him?

I am. Look, it's not safe for me to do this right now, but I'll put some information together. Contact me in a week to set up a dead drop.

>>>There is a 93.9% probability that Sigler will pursue further action against Brainstorm. The need for this information is urgent.

I'll get it to you.

Graham Brown read the text message reply. He deleted it without responding and put his smartphone away.

A week after the destruction of the facility site in Algeria…

a week after Jack Sigler had showed up to ruin the most audacious enterprise he had ever conceived…he found that he still could not keep the anger and desperation from creeping into his Brainstorm communiqués. He had spent decades cultivating the myth that Brainstorm was something larger-than-life; a sentient, even omniscient computer, and not just an ordinary—*well, maybe extraordinary*—gambler from Atlantic City with an uncanny ability to accurately assess the probabilities of almost any event.

"Pay no attention to that man behind the curtain," he muttered.

Like the Wizard of Oz, his real power wasn't his genius, but the illusion that he was something more than human. Maintaining that illusion required him to behave like a computer, to be logical and emotionless when interacting with the men and women whose service and loyalty he had surreptitiously purchased over the course of thirty years.

That kind of clinical detachment hadn't been a problem for him until Jack Sigler entered into the picture. Fortunately, there was an easy solution.

Kill Jack Sigler.

ABOUT THE AUTHORS

JEREMY ROBINSON is the author of eleven novels including PULSE, INSTINCT, and THRESHOLD the first three books in his exciting Jack Sigler series. His novels have been translated into nine languages. He is also the director of New Hampshire AuthorFest, a non-profit organization promoting literacy. He lives in New Hampshire with his wife and three children.

Visit him on the web, here:
www.jeremyrobinsononline.com

SEAN ELLIS is the author of several novels. He is a veteran of Operation Enduring Freedom, and has a Bachelor of Science degree in Natural Resources Policy from Oregon State University. He lives in Arizona, where he divides his time between writing, adventure sports, and trying to figure out how to save the world.

Visit him on the web, here:
seanellisthrillers.webs.com

COMING IN 2011

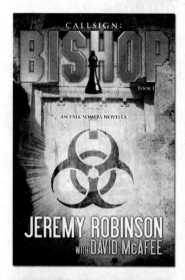

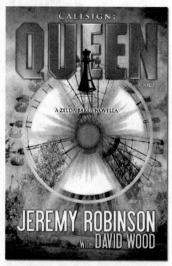

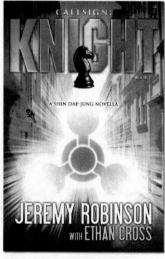

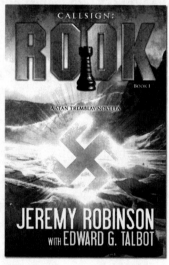